WHEN LOVE RIDES OUT

WHEN LOVE RIDES OUT

Helen McCabe

Chivers Press
Bath, England

•

Thorndike Press
Waterville, Maine USA

This Large Print edition is published by Chivers Press, England, and by Thorndike Press, USA.

Published in 2002 in the U.K. by arrangement with the author.

Published in 2002 in the U.S. by arrangement with Helen McCabe.

U.K. Hardcover ISBN 0–7540–7431–5 (Chivers Large Print)
U.S. Softcover ISBN 0–7862–4500–X (Nightingale Series Edition)

The text of this Large Print edition is unabridged.
Other aspects of the book may vary from the original edition.

Set in 16 pt. New Times Roman.

Printed in Great Britain on acid-free paper.

British Library Cataloguing in Publication Data available

Library of Congress Cataloging-in-Publication Data

McCabe, Helen, 1942–
When love rides out / by Helen McCabe.
p. cm.
ISBN 0–7862–4500–X (lg. print : sc : alk. paper)
1. Large type books. I. Title.
PR6113.C35 W48 2002
823'.92—dc21 2002020484

CHAPTER ONE

France, 1719

I wish I could go with you, Jean,' Sylvie said enviously as they pulled up their horses at the Cross, where four chalk-white dusty roads broadened out to lead to the wonderful Chateau of Chantilly.

'I wish you could, too, Sylvie,' her kinsman replied, 'but your time will come soon.'

He looked up at the girl with admiration. He and Nadine had done a good job bringing her up. Sylvie had deep auburn hair and a creamy skin. And her eyes! They were glorious like tiger stone, and how they blazed when she was angry.

'Never mind,' she said regretfully. 'I'll spend the morning as I planned in the forest. I promise I will ride home at noon.'

That day, all the best artists in Europe were to be at Chantilly for a meeting with Monsieur le Duc, great-grandson of the Prince of Condé. She longed to go with Jean to present their designs for le Duc's stables, but architecture was a man's task, even though she had helped her cousin. There were female painters in France, but very few sculptors and architects.

'You will take care?' Jean asked.

There were many rough men about these

days. France was not the place it had been when he was young. Then, the middle-aged Sun King had lavished great praise on artists and craftsmen but, now, there was famine and despair. He could still remember the serious food riots of ten years ago and the harsh winter of 1709 when Louis had ordered acres of forest to be cut down so that the poor could, at least, have wood to burn.

Louis XIV had reigned for fifty-four years, many of them in adversity and sorrow and, when he died, the people of France were glad, and heard to mutter his reign had been too long with its war and financial excesses. Perhaps the nine-year-old Louis XV could bring them all hope. But he was still a child under the regency of Philip of Orleans, the old king's nephew.

'Don't look so worried, Jean.'

Sylvie was not easily frightened.

'I have Gaston to take care of me, too.'

They both knew the boy was a goose, but a faithful one. However, unless Jean won the prize for designing the Condé stables, they could not afford new serving men. Just looking at Sylvie brought a lump to his throat. Was this the frightened, little girl he had brought to Chateau Aubade from court ten years ago to make her home with them?

'Just do your best,' she added. 'For all his faults, Monsieur le Duc knows talent when he sees it. And I feel sure you will win the competition.'

He knew she had a passionate heart, and she had grown into such a beauty. Today, her slender body was encased in her old green riding habit. She looked a picture in it but if he won, she could have all the new clothes in France. Now that his dear Nadine was dead, every ounce of his gold would be lavished on Sylvie. But had she any desire for gowns or money? She was an artist like himself, who cared nothing for show, but searched for the beauty within.

'I will,' he said determinedly, turning to look at their servants behind, manning the two carts that held the plaster models, covered to protect them from the dust.

'Look, Jean, isn't it wonderful?' Sylvie cried, pointing her whip at the open sky, rolling its clouds over the great chateau.

Dawn had broken now and, suddenly, the forest around them was full of the sweet sound of songbirds. There was a great traffic of carts and people coming out of the forests on to the Cross, making their way, like him, to attempt an audience with a man who was interested in little else but the creation of beautiful buildings and the comfort of his horses!

'I must go,' he said, 'or Hildebrant and his Germans will be there before me, or the Italians!'

Jean feared them winning, more than any of his other rivals. Many years ago, Louis XIV had invited Romano Bernini to Paris to help design his palace at Versailles. Since then the Italians had taken the upper hand with their styles. Besides, Jean wanted to build the best stables in the world at Chantilly. It was said the old king had been very jealous of the chateau built by the Prince of Condé, great-grandfather of le Duc, and that jealousy had spurred him on to try and outdo its glory at his own palace of Versailles.

'And you take care,' Sylvie said, patting his arm, 'while I am gathering my flowers. I must do it today while the weather holds. The frieze I am working on is nearly finished and then I can get on with my horses. Thank you, dear Jean, for giving me the chance to work on them.'

She was sculpting the beasts in the finest Italian marble, which had cost him what he could ill afford. But they were marble horses to die for, wonderful animals which, when they were finished, would hopefully adorn the entrance to the new stables, and guard the gates for all eternity. It was her greatest ambition!

'Oh, you and your horses,' he said, to cover the deep love he felt for her. 'When we are rich, I will buy you a mount which will far outstrip your dear old Pelotte.'

'No, Jean, I love him,' she said, patting her small piebald's neck. 'But I would not say no to your offer when we are rich. And then, poor, good Pelotte can be turned out to grass.'

They laughed companionably and her tawny eyes danced with amusement. Some moments later, Sylvie sat watching the small procession of carts, headed by Jean, proceed down the broad avenue through the parkland, which led to the grand chateau.

Near noon, the brazen sound of a distant hunting horn shattered her morning's solitude. Sylvie, startled, let go the ribbon she was tying around the bunch of wild flowers and stared in the direction of the sound. It meant there were men nearby. She had not the slightest fear of the male sex in general, only one. But no-one knew the terrible dilemma she faced, and certainly not Jean.

She breathed in deeply to calm herself. If Guy de Barre came searching for her, he would hardly find her. She was too well concealed, encircled by a mass of trees, intertwined by ivy creeper and undergrowth. She picked up the ribbon and resumed her task, but her fingers were shaking so much she could not tie the knot.

Doubts besieged her. Could de Barre have discovered her secret place, hidden so deep in the woods? After all, it was only ten miles from Chantilly. The great forest held no natural terrors for Sylvie, even though her father had met a mysterious death there. This glade, five miles from Chateau Aubade, was in its very depths. It had been her special place from childhood, full of thickets, mossy watery holes and wild beasts. But at eighteen, the animal Sylvie despised most was human. Guy de Barre was a close adviser to le Duc. He could be a powerful ally or a dangerous enemy, and she hated him.

It was common knowledge at Chantilly that he had desired her for years. That was why Monsieur le Duc had placed the eight-year-old Sylvie into Jean's care and protection. Now she was grown, she was wary but, that day, she had sent Gaston away. Jean would not have approved, but, as an artist, too, he would have understood why Sylvie wished to keep her hideaway secret. For here, the wild flowers and plants grew in lush profusion. Today, she was gathering them as studies for her painting. She did not want horses' hooves disturbing them.

The day was very warm for May and the heavy canopy of trees ensured her fair complexion was not at risk of burning. In fact, Sylvie had taken off her hat and left it dangling from its ribbons on a branch. She listened for the horn again, but she could only hear the birds. She concluded she must be safe, after all, and began to gather her things.

She wondered how Jean was faring. Had he managed an audience with Monsieur le Duc, and would Madame Baptiste be present at the Court that morning? Sylvie frowned, thinking about Elise.

Madame Elise was a lady of fashion, a

wealthy widow, who had recently come to Chantilly from the boy king's court at Versailles. She was an accomplished portrait painter, who had been invited by le Duc to portray him. Privately, Sylvie felt Jean was more impressed by the lady's manners and appearance, but would never have told him so openly. On the few occasions she had been in Elise's company, Sylvie had felt particularly young and naïve in comparison with the lady's worldly sophistication.

She was resolved to be civil to her as a fellow artist, and for Jean's sake but, secretly, she could not entertain the idea of her taking Nadine's place. She sighed. She missed Jean's dear wife so much. She had been snatched away by the evil smallpox at only thirty-four years of age. They had been such good friends and, although she would not wish Jean to be alone always, he would scarcely find a wife again of such quality.

Suddenly, the horn assailed her ears again. She stood up tall and pushed back her heavy hair. Then she clenched her fists. Sylvie possessed Jean's courage and determination in adversity. No hunter or peasant would harm her in the Chantilly forest. The locals held le Duc in awe, and anyone who did evil towards those he favoured paid dearly.

Sylvie wore a ribbon on her breast to show she had a part in the stables competition. The Condé's crest was well known in the villages around. But if it was de Barre who was hunting for her, she must show no fear; only the will to resist him, as strong as his to possess her.

She thrust the last and the most fragile, hastily-gathered wood anemones into the open lacing of her dark green bodice, glad she was wearing riding apparel and not her hooped skirt, which was no good in a hurry. Sylvie then hurried over to Pelotte. The piebald had been cropping the sweet herb-strewn grass contentedly. Now he was restive, so she stroked his nose soothingly.

It was far too late to mount and flee from the glade, so she stood with her back pressed against a sturdy trunk, her breathing rapid as the riders approached. Then faithful Pelotte started, wrenching her fingers back. Although the piebald was old, he still had spirit.

'Steady,' she whispered, but, innocently, the faithful horse had revealed her hiding place.

Suddenly, the riders, accompanied by huge, rough dogs, burst through, damaging her private glade, filling it with raucous sounds. Next moment, Pelotte whinnied in panic and galloped from the glade, cutting off any chance for Sylvie to escape. The leader dug in his spurs and brought his mount, lathered with sweat and foaming at the mouth, to an abrupt halt. It was de Barre, and he was laughing! Her whole body shook with contempt.

'Sylvie!'

'Monsieur!'

Her hazel eyes blazed as she regarded him steadily. He was controlling his plunging horse with the star-shaped spurs of his heavy jackboots.

'Can a girl not gather flowers without being disturbed by a pack of hounds?' she exclaimed as Guy de Barre dismounted.

'Stand off,' he ordered his men who obeyed, retreating to a distance.

Sylvie eyed her tormentor warily. She had always thought him ugly.

'I've called off my dogs, Sylvie. Does that please you?' he asked, smiling, but his eyes glittered coldly, like a venomous snake. 'You took some finding,' he said.

Sylvie's stomach turned. Her suspicions had been right. This meeting had been no accident.

'You should take care. As I have told you often, being alone in the forest is dangerous for a young woman,' he continued.

'Not for me,' she retorted. 'I know it well. Besides, Gaston is nearby.'

She needed to lie, to remind de Barre that he was the danger and help was not far off. He unfastened the clasp of his short riding cloak. Beneath, he wore black hunting garb, spattered with forest mud but, on his chest, bright jewels flashed.

'Soon, Sylvie, you will be decked out richly, too,' he said, 'if my master grants your kinsman his great commission.'

'I am not interested in gems, monsieur, only

that Jean will make the most of his opportunities,' she retorted.

'A pity that these are the only jewels you possess.'

His eyes were fixed on the frail anemones, nestling at her bosom.

'But things could change.'

He stretched out a beringed hand and she stiffened with disgust.

'You are like a wood nymph with your wild red hair and ivory skin,' he added softly.

'What do you want with me, monsieur?'

'To offer you a proposition. It concerns Aubade.'

'Then speak with him about it.'

'It is a delicate matter, and needs your swift agreement.'

'What do you mean?'

'You care about him? You wish him success in his ventures?'

'You speak in riddles, monsieur! Say what you mean and be done!'

He caught her wrist and imprisoned it. She winced, and struggled to release herself.

'You're hurting me!'

'Then listen, Sylvie, and stop play acting. Aubade thinks he has the edge with le Duc now,' he persisted, 'but there are many others, experienced architects from all over Europe, young aristocrats, who would give their right arms to design the greatest stables in France for the noble Monsieur le Duc.'

He was now very close to her face and she could smell his foul breath.

'I promise that the commission for the great stables would come faster and to the right place if you took yourself a powerful suitor to speak up for your dear Jean,' he hissed.

She loathed de Barre now more than she had ever done. She remembered how, as a child, she had cried with relief when, on le Duc's orders, Jean had accepted her under his protection. Her eyes smarted with tears. Jean knew how much she hated de Barre and would do his best to protect her. Although the man pretended he had known and loved her dead parents, his attentions had been the bane of her childhood. But Jean needed to be careful. Now de Barre was ready to use her love for Jean as a weapon in his own favour. He clearly thought she would submit to his blackmail.

'Jean does not need any champion,' she said clearly. 'His designs speak for themselves and Monsieur de Duc knows that well!'

'Brave words, Sylvie,' de Barre sneered, 'but you may need my help before long. Mark my words, if you don't fall in with me, I shall see that you and your kinsman fall out with my master. Every artist needs a patron, however well he is connected. Aubade is no different. Shall I let you into a secret?' he whispered.

As he leaned forward conspiratorially, he saw her recoil.

'Your precious Jean has a young and

powerful rival, come hotfoot from the king's court at Versailles. You may have heard of him, Yves, Marquis de Sainton!' he snarled. 'A fine young aristocrat, who will be set highest of all in le Duc's estimation, if you deny me what I want more than life itself.'

His cold lips pressed down on her palm.

'Impoverished you may be, but it is in my power to restore your lands. And you know it, Sylvie!'

Sylvie shuddered.

'You're a brute, de Barre,' she cried. 'I will never give in to your desires. I will tell Jean what you have said and done. He is not afraid of you, nor this marquis of whom you speak.'

Her eyes blazed indignantly at him but, inside, she felt real fear. He laughed mockingly.

'I would not hurt you, Sylvie. You'll come to me willingly. I vow you will be begging me before I have finished. Think on what I said. You have a short time, a brief space only, to come to your senses.'

His narrow face shrivelled into an ugly mask. The thought of a marriage alliance with Guy de Barre was abhorrent. Sylvie knew le Duc had her welfare at heart but he trusted de Barre and, if the monster asked for her hand formally, there was a chance his request would be granted. Her oppressor was rich and it would be a good match.

Also, if she submitted, she would be

reclaiming lands that were rightfully hers. It was a monstrous hurt to Sylvie that a great part of the St Berthaud estates had been bestowed upon de Barre by the old king, when her father was disgraced and fled to the court at Chantilly. But, even though personally she was penniless and fatherless, deprived of her birthright by her father's treacherous enemies who were still unknown and unpunished, she still had Jean on her side. He would resist this suit with all his strength, even though he needed the commission so greatly.

'I can see you are thinking about my offer.'

De Barre's voice was rough no longer, only silken with longing.

'I have thought already,' Sylvie retorted. 'Your offer can putrefy. Its rotten stink offends me and this place. Leave my sight!'

His eyes flicked wide with surprise, then his nostrils flared in anger. He stood motionless. If he had been going to seize her, he would have done so by now! He laughed.

'I don't want to break your spirit, Sylvie. When your eyes blaze out like that, you remind me of your dear mother, Victoire. She was a tigress, too, so beautiful when she was angry!'

Sylvie clenched her small fists. She had never known her maman, who had died giving her life.

'Don't you dare insult my mother!'

'You think me cruel? Then that is good. At

least, you think something of me, and I will not give up, I promise you. My offer stands and will for some months. But, in the end, I will lose patience. Goodbye, Sylvie, and let me see the results of your labours when they are ready to show.'

He flicked the frail anemones with his fingers. She averted her head and he turned impatiently on his heel and mounted, gesturing imperiously to the rest of his men.

'Gaston will soon be here to rescue you!'

Next moment, he was galloping from the glade, his men behind him. Sylvie closed her eyes in relief, leaning back against the warm bark. Anger overcame her. She hated Guy de Barre, with all her heart. Would she never be rid of the man who plagued her now as much as he had in her childhood? But she'd never submit. Never!

A moment later, she was starting up as tree branches and bushes swished. More riders? Had de Barre come back? She stood to face them, knowing this time she might not be so lucky. Then a great black horse crashed into her glade. Sylvie stared at the arrogant, dark-eyed stranger, his full lips tightening into a hard line with the effort of reining in his thoroughbred mount. In a minute he had it under control. Was he one of de Barre's followers returned to overpower her?

CHAPTER TWO

Mam'selle, is this your horse?' he demanded, pointing imperiously, and she could hardly believe her eyes as she spied the small, subdued Pelotte, running behind his own magnificent stallion.

He stared down at her, his lips curling arrogantly, while his bold, dark eyes raked her body rudely. She challenged the look, but her stomach was churning. His quizzical expression demanded a response!

'Why do you think that is my mount?' Sylvie's voice rang out bravely.

'I hope the beast is yours, mam'selle, or there is some other female lying untended in the woods,' he bantered, indicating the side-saddle. 'But I have more precious matters to attend to with my time than rescuing pretty women and capturing aged horses.'

He eyed old Pelotte so scornfully that Sylvie bristled.

'How did you find me?' she accused.

'Find you? I did not find you, but instead, your horse.'

She could see he did not lack wit.

'The beast almost brought me down, and being riderless, I decided to look for whoever had been unseated. I am not given to acts of charity.'

He shrugged his shoulders carelessly, then leaned over his saddle pommel.

'But, from henceforth, I will be searching for every runaway animal who might lead me to some other grateful victim.'

Although his sarcasm bit hard, his steady gaze was lingering on her face, caressing it. She had never experienced such a look. To cover her confusion, she snapped back at him.

'Don't sport with me, sir. How did you find my secret place?'

'Secret? Ah,' he said with a smile, ignoring her last question. 'So this glade belongs to you? I was under the impression the forest was the property of the Prince of Condé, Monsieur le Duc.'

'On licence from the King of France!' Sylvie retorted.

'You have a knowledge of the law as well?' he countered as he swung his booted leg over his horse and dismounted.

Seated high on a horse gave a man supremacy over an adversary but, as the stranger approached, she became fully aware by the hot look in his eyes he might be just as dangerous on the ground. Her lips went dry and she moistened them with her tongue. She could see he had the stride of the military as well as the lithe build of the soldier as he brought Pelotte over.

'You study me, mam'selle?' he asked.

He thought she was an extraordinarily good-looking girl with her auburn hair and translucent skin, the colour of alabaster. He was glad he had rescued her.

'Keep away, sir,' she said, 'or you will suffer some harm.'

His lips twitched with that infuriating, tantalising smile.

'Harm? You have a dagger?'

How he longed suddenly to slip his arm about her. His eyes lingered on the Condé ribbon. What a sweet rival she would make!

Sylvie found his steady gaze unnerving. She averted her eyes. She was thinking his eyes were the most roguish she had ever seen.

'If I keep away from you, mam'selle, how will you retrieve your horse?'

There was scarcely an arm's length between them now.

'Now, stab me, mam'selle, if you dare. But only with your eyes!'

His lips curled once more into that maddening smile.

'You are insufferable, sir,' she retorted hotly. 'And no gentleman.'

She saw he did not like that, because his expression darkened.

'Then you would rather I left you here in the forest at the wild boar's mercy?'

'I have no fear of the boar, sir, only human animals.'

'You are ungrateful, mam'selle,' he replied.

She could see his mouth twitching. He had a

temper, too, but a tiny voice in her head was telling her this was the most handsome man she had ever seen but at the same time warning her that, often, such charming males could be cruel.

She reached out her hand to take Pelotte's rein and touched his fingers. A hot shiver stung her body like tongues of fire. Sylvie snatched the reins out of his hand and tried to mount, but to her dismay, Pelotte bucked and shifted in his excitement, leaving her feet dangling in the most unladylike position.

Her body stiffened at the stranger's laugh then, to her shame, she felt his strong, warm hand hitch her stockinged leg over the side-saddle horn. Then another shoved her into the saddle. Next moment, she was up and erect, and he was standing below, mocking her. He thought she looked like a May-time goddess in her green habit with her wild red hair in disarray and the drooping white flowers still at her breast. How he longed to worship her!

'You are no gentleman, sir!' she panted.

He must defend himself on that charge. It was quite untrue.

'And I say you can be no lady,' he retorted, wanting to see her roused, 'all alone in the forest with no-one to chaperone you.'

'How dare you!' she cried, wresting her short whip from the saddlebag.

He caught her reins with one hand and, as she rained down blows, he grasped the whip and broke it over his knee.

'I dare, mam'selle,' he shouted, 'because Yves, Marquis of Sainton, has never struck a woman, but allows no woman to strike him!'

His voice was as hard as his eyes, yet her wildcat beauty thrilled him.

Sylvie's breath stabbed her chest at the name. He was the toady of de Barre, and her hated rival. A cold thrill passed through her body.

'Then you think too much of yourself, sir,' she cried, wheeling Pelotte around. 'I will strike whom I please, and any man who mishandles me, especially a follower of Guy de Barre!'

She spurred Pelotte into a canter.

Yves Sainton was taken by surprise at her sudden departure. Then, throwing down her broken whip, he ran rapidly towards his own horse.

Sylvie dashed on madly through the glade, ducking overhanging branches, smashing through the undergrowth, making for the openings in the trees, which led to the network of forest paths bringing her close to home. Recent storms had made the ground heavy underfoot and clumsy Pelotte was no match for the spirited black stallion.

The wind in her ears carried the sound of the thudding hooves behind her, and they were getting nearer. She was forced to zigzag, trying to lose him and kept making for home. At least her pursuer would not dare follow her into her own chateau. It was a long, mad chase and testament to the skill of both the riders, but Pelotte was nearly dead on his feet as she cried out with relief when she saw another rider coming from the opposite direction. She galloped to meet the familiar figure.

'Gaston,' she shouted. 'Gaston! Here I am. Hold! Hold!'

He stopped. Next moment, she was beside him, hot tears mixing with the spattered mud on her cheeks. The young groom's face was white as he faced her determined pursuer bravely. Seated beside him, Sylvie gasped at the shameful sight. The marquis' bright sword was drawn and, dangling from its point by its ribbons was her old hat! The man's sensuous lips were twitching as he brandished his blade and the sorry object.

'This time it was your hat you lost, my lady!'

He laughed.

'But 'tis not harmed. Well, only a trifle. Here! Take it, boy.'

The serving lad's face was very pale, faced with the blade's sharp point. Sylvie's eyes flashed. The man was almost as odious as de Barre, revelling in their joint humiliation. A subdued Gaston awaited her orders miserably.

'Take it!' she hissed through clenched teeth.

Gaston grasped the hat gingerly. A grinning Sainton sheathed his glittering sword. Then, eyes dancing with mirth, he bowed briefly, and cantered away without a backward glance.

Sylvie's cheeks were flaming. Snatching the offending headgear from Gaston's trembling fingers, she hurled it into the bushes.

'Mark my words, I will make that gentleman suffer. But he is no gentleman.'

With that, she kicked old Pelotte's fat sides, and, finding a new reserve of strength within him, after his short rest, he snorted indignantly and trotted off as fast as he could, closely followed by a white-faced Gaston.

Still smarting from her encounter, Sylvie reined in the weary Pelotte at the edge of the woods which protected Chateau Aubade. Looking down the hill and across a single cornfield, she could see its roofs thrusting fairy-like to the sky, its twin turrets and warm stone shining out like a honeyed beacon, windows gleaming in the sun.

This charming chateau had been built by one of Jean's clerical ancestors, to house his secret mistress. Then, the Aubades had been rich and when Jean's forbear was pursued by the lady's irate husband the wily priest had managed to overcome the angry spouse and imprison him in the turret tower which, now, was Sylvie's bedroom.

In those days, Chateau Aubade had not been neglected, but, at present, in spite of their many efforts, parts of it were crumbling, some of its roofs were covered in moss and its woodwork was cracking in a thousand places.

As she and Gaston rode down the hill towards the moat, she thought for the hundredth time how much they needed to win that prize and pocket Condé's gold.

But Aubade was still beautiful and welcoming. As they crossed the narrow bridge across the moat, she caught her breath. Within the courtyard stood the smartest of carriages, attended by liveried flunkies. Sylvie recognised the arms on the side of the coach—Madame Elise was visiting! For the first time that stressful morning, Sylvie worried about her appearance. She must look more like a peasant wench than the last of the noble St Berthauds! She must get dressed up before Madame Elise beheld her. She would enter the chateau from the back and steal up to her turret bedroom unnoticed.

Turning Pelotte's head, she urged him through the side gate and round towards the stables where their workshops lay. Once there, she was shocked. The courtyard was full of strange servants, piling up carts with their tools and, to her horror, the heavy dust sheets had been lifted from her marble blocks, exposing her unfinished horse sculptures. She panicked. What dreadful trouble had come upon them, and where was Jean?

She wheeled Pelotte around.

'Come here,' she ordered a workman. 'What are you doing with that marble?'

'We are moving it, my lady.'

Sylvie's eyes blazed.

'On whose authority?'

'On Monsieur le Duc's.'

'Oh, no!' Sylvie cried, launching herself from Pelotte's back and next moment, charging across the courtyard madly.

'Sylvie!' Jean exclaimed, arching his eyebrows.

He was standing with his back to the fireplace, wearing his comfortable loose gown, with the front wrapped over. She ran right up to him.

'Jean, what is happening? Why are they moving all our things?'

'Calm yourself, dear,' Jean said, patting her arm. 'There is no cause for such alarm. It is good news. It is le Duc's orders, and Madame Elise is as glad to hear it as we are.'

'Good news?' she repeated, her head whirling.

A moment later, she came back to herself and remembered what a fright she looked, suddenly aware of the sophisticated woman seated elegantly beside the fireplace, regarding her sympathetically.

What would Elise Baptiste think of her, behaving like a hoyden rather than an elegant, young lady? But she did not seem to have noticed, because she was smiling kindly.

'Great news,' Jean added. 'Monsieur le Duc has been kind enough to place my design in the second round, with the Italians, and we will beat them, Sylvie, with their twirls and rococo cherubs. He has given orders that, from now on, we may continue our work at Court. It's a grand compliment. We shall have all the advantages, and the materials to continue. We'll have our own workshop there.'

Jean was like a delighted little boy.

'I am so happy for you,' a dazed Sylvie said.

'Are you ill, my dear?' Madame Elise asked. 'You seem quite overwrought.'

'No, thank you, I am not,' Sylvie sobbed. 'Forgive me both. I will go to my chamber. I am only tired from riding so hard, because I was late.'

Now was not the time to tell Jean about her encounter with Guy de Barre, nor of her other with his henchman, the Marquis of Sainton.

A very different Sylvie descended the staircase later in a hooped gown of sky blue, opening in the front to reveal a silken petticoat of a darker hue. The bodice was boned and tight-fitting and the front left open to reveal a modest cleavage. She was satisfied that now she looked a lady but, inside, she felt less than calm. Under the light of one hundred candles, they sat down to dinner. Madame Elise, exquisite in an evening gown of moonlight satin, leaned forward.

'You look wonderful, my dear.'

She smiled across the table.

'Jean, she will be a sensation at Court. How long since you have been there, Sylvie?'

'Some time now,' she said truthfully and, in fact, she was glad to keep away, in case she was molested by de Barre. 'I do not care for life at Court,' she added.

Madame's laugh was like a tinkling bell.

'Then we must change your mind, my dear. There are so many handsome youths to meet, who will be eagerly attentive. It could be the finest time of your life.'

'I would rather sculpt my horses,' Sylvie replied truthfully.

'But you shall, and meet young aristocrats. I will introduce you.'

She addressed her next words to Jean.

'She must be in my sole care.'

He nodded. Sylvie could see he was fascinated by the lady, and would agree to almost anything.

'Together, your fair cousin and I will make men know that women artists are more than dabblers.'

Sylvie continued to watch her kinsman's face as Madame Elise prattled on. She could see he was truly smitten. Madame Elise was kind. Should she confide in her? But Sylvie resolved to keep her counsel at present. Toying with her food, she listened idly to them talking of Chantilly.

'And you met another rival, too? Yves, Marquis of Sainton?' Madame said and Sylvie listened carefully.

'I did,' Jean said. 'He was one of the first to

show. He is a queer, cool fish, for one so young. While Monsieur le Duc was looking at his design, the man was attending to his nails, as if he could not care less about the competition. Then he was off, without a by-your-leave.'

'That sounds like him,' madame cried. 'Yves can be such a popinjay. He never used to be. His fame as a soldier is very well known. He comes from a very old military family, noted for their bravery.'

'Do you know the marquis then?' Sylvie asked, alert now.

'Not well, but enough. I have met his mother, but, when I was painting at Versailles, I would chance upon him sometimes, careering around the corridors like some mad horse, with the young King upon his back.'

'Upon his back?' Jean and Sylvie gasped together.

'Oh, yes.' Elise laughed. 'He is the King's favourite playmate. He makes him laugh and the boy has little to laugh about, burdened as he is with affairs of state at such a tender age. He has Sainton beside him morning to night. He calls him my pretty horse, and what young Louis will do with the fellow gone, I cannot imagine.'

'Why did he leave then, seeing he is in such great favour with the King?' Sylvie asked.

'He is an accomplished architect, taught and trained by the greatest master in France, and he has a will on him like iron. He couldn't have borne it if his work on the stables had not been taken into account. They say that if he does not win the prize, he will go mad.'

Sylvie was thinking of those dangerous, dark eyes, which had strafed her body. He would be a fearsome rival. But, if he was such a favourite with the King, how did he get mixed up with de Barre? Surely he would not need that toad's patronage?

'And has he a noble patron in Condé's Court?' she pried.

'He needs no-one. He is wealthy enough. He has estates throughout France but after his father was killed in the Spanish wars, his mother, Angèle, took a great house, west of Paris, so she could be near to her son in Versailles. I have met her several times. She is a very great lady.'

Madame Elise lowered her voice.

'As for the marquis, who is so close to the King, the rumour is that wily Guy de Barre has taken him under his wing so that he can curry favour with the King.'

Jean snorted and his eyes flashed.

'That sounds about right!'

'But Yves is both clever and circumspect and must see de Barre for what he is, I believe,' Madame Elise replied, sipping her wine. 'But, there, I do not know. It is a mystery why he likes that man.'

She put down her glass. Sylvie could tell by

her tone that she had no time for de Barre. Then, Elise's eyes were gleaming, as if a new idea had struck her suddenly.

'I will introduce you to the marquis, Sylvie. He may be Jean's rival but you can make up your own mind about him. I am sure you and he will have much in common. You are both exceedingly handsome, and both artists.'

Sylvie's heart leaped. She wanted to cry out that not only had she met Sainton already, but that he had treated her despicably and he could not be trusted. He was in league with de Barre! But she did neither, tormented by the memory. And, also, although it greatly confused and ashamed her, the thought of meeting him again sent a delicious thrill through her whole body. She squashed the unfamiliar feeling immediately.

'What do you think, Jean? Should the young people meet?' Elise added.

Sylvie blushed for both of them, as well as for herself, and drank deeply from her goblet to cover her confusion. She never wanted to see Yves Sainton again, after his boorish behaviour, but that little voice had returned once more to her head telling her she was lying. She put down her glass and rose from the table.

'I would like to retire now,' she announced. 'If you will excuse me?'

'Good idea,' Jean replied. 'Then you will be refreshed and ready for an early start.

Madame and I still have much to discuss, about the art of painting,' he added.

As Sylvie left the dining-room, she could hear Elise's bell-like laughter trilling down the corridor. She told herself she did not mind. In truth, her heart was full of another laugh, a deeper sound, which tantalisingly mocked her heated senses.

CHAPTER THREE

Sylvie gazed around in awe. She had been in Chantilly a day already. Her marble horses had been safely installed, as had Jean's initial plaster models. His others were under wraps in his rooms. Secrecy had to be maintained as his rivals were jealous men.

She looked up. In the twilight, the huge, vaulted roof of their new studio was dim. The workshop, situated near the old moat, was magnificent. None of their rivals had such a congenial place in which to work.

She had told her new maidservant she wished to walk abroad alone and the girl had looked at her with frightened eyes. Sylvie did not think her sudden decision to visit the new workshop had been rash. She was not afraid of forest wildernesses, so why should she fear a short walk in this civilised place, going from her apartment to her studio.

In fact, in spite of Madame Baptiste's attempts to prevail upon her to meet young men, she was nervous of mingling with the courtiers in the mirrored grand salon where the chevaliers strode about in their finery. Jean had closeted himself in his rooms, to study the second stage of his designs, to be ready for tomorrow and, Elise, herself, had gone early to her rooms. So, Sylvie had the evening free and the place all to herself.

Her eyes lingered, satisfied, on the huge, draped blocks of marble, which had been hauled into a place of honour, on a large dais with ladders and scaffolding from which she could work unhindered. As she walked slowly towards her handiwork, the train of her dress dragging behind her through the dust, she thrilled at what lay under those heavy dust sheets.

She longed to go up the ladder and pull the cloths away, to take her hammer and chisel and continue. Instead, she contented herself by touching the dust sheets, knowing her tableau was safe beneath. She yawned again. She must sleep or she would be good for nothing tomorrow.

Monsieur le Duc had appointed it the day to ride out with his teams of architects and review the site set aside for the great stables. Le Duc had told Jean he had plans to stable over two hundred horses and five hundred hounds there. She was so tired she didn't hear the footsteps coming up behind her! Next moment, she almost screamed at the light touch on her shoulder, and swung round in the gloom.

Those hot eyes proclaimed the man's identity—the Marquis of Sainton. She looked away quickly.

'Sir,' she gasped. 'What are you doing here? How did you find me?'

'I have heard that speech from you before, Sylvie! Am I trespassing again?' he asked with a laugh.

Her cheeks reddened.

'You are indelicate, sir, to remind me of our past unfortunate encounter. Anyway, how do you know my name? We have not been introduced!'

'Not formally, I grant you, but . . .'

His eyes lingered on her lovely face, and his voice softened.

'Who has not heard of Sylvie St Berthaud and her wonderful, marble horses.'

Anger suffused her. He could mock her personally, but not her art.

'So you are acquainted with my sculpture, sir?' she said coldly.

She must be on her guard. He was probably de Barre's spy! He shook his head and, leaving her side, strode over to the dais. She thought of what she had heard about him—a fighting man turned fop.

'Are these your horses? I was hoping to see

them.'

He stood, his back to her, looking up at the dust sheets. She stared at the width of his broad shoulders. She was thinking of Elise's words and she blushed unseen at the thought of the boy King, clinging to his back as he rode him through the corridors of Versailles. How would that feel? Sylvie's knowledge of male ways had come through listening to the prattle of chambermaids about the sport of love. She had no mother, nor any close girl friends. Besides, real ladies did not speak wantonly of the male sex. Because of this and de Barre's unwelcome attentions, she had always been cool to the few gentlemen she had met, not trusting any of them. But this one—was he the same?

She clenched her fists by her side to quell her reckless thoughts, ashamed of them. The marquis brought feelings to her body that left her legs weak. But he was no different from other men. He might even be worse. He had to be, if he associated with de Barre.

'How much have you done?' he said as he turned round, put his hands on his hips and smiled. 'You are determined not to tell me, are you? So, like the rest of us, you are jealous!'

'What do you mean?' she snapped.

If only someone understood her!

'Well, I am an artist myself and I would not dream of showing my handiwork to any, except of course, my dearest friends.'

She bristled.

'Then you will never see my horses, sir.'

'Harsh words,' he answered quizzically, putting a hand over his heart. 'I am wounded, mam'selle. Does this mean you do not like me? Or are you afraid I will steal your ideas? Don't worry. I am no sculptor. I cannot work in marble. I draw plans. There lies my interest. Oh, Sylvie, I have such plans.'

He threw open his arms expansively and stretched like some lazy lion. If he had not been as dismissive of sculpture, not one of de Barre's toadies, she would have loved to hear what his dreams were, but she kept her own lips tight. Moving swiftly towards her, he touched her mouth lightly with the tip of his finger. She jumped back, sizzling from that touch.

'Sweet lips were made for kissing, Sylvie, not for grimaces,' he quipped.

Doubtless, by the look on his face, he was speaking from wide experience. To how many women had he said that? No man would get near to Sylvie St Berthaud, unless she truly loved him. The word struck her heart like a dagger. Whom would she love? Whom could she trust? Those whom she had loved, she was doomed to lose, like Nadine and her dear parents. Her eyes flashed.

'I should not be here,' she said. 'And you neither! You should not have touched me. It was unforgivable.'

'Only your lips, mam'selle, and in sport. I beg your pardon,' he said.

His eyes were full of honesty, but an angry Sylvie thought this a sham.

'This is the Court and many assignations take place under cover of darkness, when chaperones are all asleep. But I have no desire to compromise you, Sylvie.'

He was now standing in front of the door. She believed he intended to cut off her retreat. She had to get away.

Yves admitted he was lying, but only to himself. His desires for this girl shouted for far more than compromise. In the forest, he had thought her like a May-time goddess, now she was Diana personified, a silvered tigress with her wild, red curls and in her golden gown. She had accused him of being no gentleman yet if he had not been one, he would have taken her in his arms by now and crushed the resistance from her lovely body. But this was Sylvie St Berthaud, a lady, who deserved more.

Sylvie made ready to go past him, afraid of what she saw in his look, in spite of her earlier bravery.

'Let me pass,' she commanded, and he pulled himself back from the brink of his feelings, unbarring her way.

'Very well, if you give me leave to escort you to your room.'

He saw alarm in her eyes.

'To keep you safe,' he added.

'No,' Sylvie cried and, picking up her skirts, charged past him.

'Wait!' he called, but she took no notice. 'I caught you before, mam'selle,' he shouted. 'And I will catch you again,' he said, his mouth twitching with amusement, as he ran. 'I shall not let you out of my sight, Sylvie, while you remain in Chantilly.'

He caught up with her at the bottom of a flight of stairs.

'You are fleet of foot, mam'selle,' he said softly. 'You almost gave me the slip.'

His warm fingers touched her arm but she pulled away.

'Please, mam'selle, I will not harm you, but others might. I beg you, let me escort you to your chamber.'

He realised she was unsure of its direction.

'It's that way,' he said, pointing.

'You know the way to my bedroom?' she accused.

'I know the chateau well, mam'selle. I have been here longer than you.'

'You are the danger,' she said, 'you and Guy de Barre.'

There was a break in her voice.

'How do you know that gentleman? What has he done to you that you speak so ill of him? And why couple me with his transgressions?'

'Like you know about me and my horses, I know about you and your liaison with him!'

He flushed with anger at the words.

'Who told you this?'

'De Barre himself! He spoke to me of you and your monstrous desire to win the competition, and how he would help you, at my cousin's expense. You see, I understand a great deal, even though I am unsure of the direction of my chamber.'

He looked so angry. But she continued wilfully, hazarding even more.

'I am not safe, sir, as you say. You may be privy to my movements, but I do not desire your attentions. I have Monsieur le Duc's, and I will call on him in my need.'

It was a caustic, angry speech.

'You have said enough, mam'selle.'

Yves pressed his full lips into a thin, hard line, a habit he had developed when women scolded him. He would not retaliate.

'Then if you will not heed my words, mam'selle, take good care of yourself and your cousin. Guard yourself and your designs without ceasing. Monsieur le Duc cannot always be present as your saviour.'

'I hear your callous threats,' Sylvie retorted, 'and I am not afraid of either you or de Barre. Jean will beat you in the competition! His plans are wonderful, and they are safe. He is working on them now in his rooms, while you are idly harassing me down here. He is worth the two of you!'

He stared calmly at her, letting her insults

rebound, like barbed arrows on pewter. The moonlight struck him. Suddenly, her torrent of passionate anger was waning. The moonlight was drawing her to him with its silken bands. Why was she feeling sorry for her outburst?

She picked up her skirts again to climb the twisting stairway, which she was certain led to her chamber. Next moment, Sainton swept into a low bow, then turned abruptly on his heel and disappeared into a door leading to Monsieur le Duc's private apartments. She climbed up the stone steps.

The man, hiding behind a statue placed in a deep recess of the courtyard, was angry. It had set Guy de Barre's teeth on edge to see Sylvie and young Sainton together. He had hoped to approach her in the studio. His spy had noted when she was alone and where she had gone, then had alerted him. But Sainton had forestalled him.

The marquis was proving troublesome. The last thing Guy wanted was for the aristocrat to succeed with Sylvie. She was his! But he and Yves must remain on good terms, if Guy was to get to the boy King's side. His eyes gleamed. He would have it all—his ambition and Sylvie. If he made Jean Aubade suffer enough, she would come round.

He had a lot to do before dawn. The Spaniards were waiting for him in their apartments. They were swarthy, cunning men, who would do anything to secure the prize. He had them all in the palm of his hand. It was good to have such power.

*   *   *

'Sylvie! Where have you been?'

To Sylvie's dismay, Elise was waiting for her in the corridor, her cap and nightgown covered with a light velvet cloak. Sylvie was mortified. She had thought Elise to be in bed. She must truly think she had been up to no good, wandering abroad alone.

'In the studio, madame,' Sylvie answered, shamefacedly.

'At this time of night? Why? You should not have gone out alone. You might have come to some harm. It was most indiscreet.'

'I know,' Sylvie replied, 'but I wanted to see my horses were safe.'

'Oh, Sylvie,' Elise said, taking her arm and leading her into her bedroom. 'You have much to learn about Court. An unaccompanied young woman is game for any drunken chevalier. You may blush,' she said, touching Sylvie's hot cheek, 'but when men meet an unchaperoned lady, they can take advantage, for they know that such an indiscreet young woman would make more a suitable mistress than a wife. Promise me you will not do it again.'

'I promise, madame,' Sylvie said, her cheeks very red.

'And, next time you wish to see your horses, ask me to accompany you, please. I promised Jean I would take care of you.'

With that, Elise kissed her warmly on both cheeks.

'Now, go to bed, Sylvie. You have an exciting day in front of you. Do you want my help to undress?'

'No, thank you, Elise.'

Elise still looked troubled when she left, and Sylvie wondered if she would tell Jean about her escapade. She sighed. She had had such great hopes of this time spent in Chantilly, but everything was going wrong. She looked round the room miserably and began to prepare herself for bed. She had no intention of waking the maid, who was sleeping next door.

She reached for her negligee. It was a light garment, which was becoming popular throughout the whole of Europe. Drawing the loosely-gathered gown about herself, she walked over to the window, which looked across the parkland. Her chamber was high on the second floor, overlooking a small spinney of tall, flowering bushes, with a stone seat beneath, guarded by two statues, whose marble bodies glimmered in the darkness.

Then Sylvie gasped as a slight figure, swathed in a hood and cloak, slipped out from the door, which must be directly underneath her room. She could see it was a woman. Next moment, a man's shape emerged from the spinney and greeted her. An assignation, such as Madame Elise had spoken of! Sylvie caught her breath as the moon came out from behind a cloud, revealing him. She had little difficulty recognising the Marquis of Sainton.

Sylvie drew back behind the drapes, afraid he would look up and catch sight of her. She was surprised at the mixture of feelings which coursed through her body. She felt like a spy and withdrew. There had been no overt impropriety between the couple, but a coldness crept over Sylvie, gripping her senses like an icy hand. What else could she expect from a man who allied himself with a rogue like de Barre?

Suddenly, Sylvie longed to know who the lady was. She thought of Elise again. What had she said about men taking mistresses? Doubtless, Sainton possessed one, or even more, given his handsome looks. But that he should meet with his love under Sylvie's window seemed quite unforgivable. She drew the heavy curtains, blotting out the sight. Throwing off her negligee, she climbed into her nightgown and up on to the high bed where, disdaining to get under the covers, she lay on top, burying her face in the goose-down pillows to blot out the memory. Some moments later, she was sound asleep.

And there she lay until dawn, only disturbed by Yves Sainton, who appeared in her dreams as he had in reality, like no gentleman.

CHAPTER FOUR

Yves Sainton stood outside one of the striped tents which had been set up in the fields to house the Court on its outing to the site. As its awnings fluttered in the light breeze, he stared across to where the groups of brightly-dressed ladies were gathered.

But Yves had eyes for only one, the auburn-headed girl, whose light green and white satin marked her out from the others. She reminded him of a rare lily amidst a cluster of overblown roses.

'A fine, young woman, Yves.'

Someone touched his elbow lightly. De Barre had come up so quietly, he hadn't noticed. Yves lifted his eyebrows questioningly and looked down at the courtier, who was inches shorter than himself. The man was dressed in his habitual black, like a churchman, but adorned with a surfeit of jewels.

'To whom do you refer?'

De Barre grinned. He was willing to go along with the young fop's pretence, and gestured.

'The pretty filly in green. I know you have your eyes set upon her. She stands out from the rest, a filly among mares, does she not?'

Yves was full of contempt at the words. De

Barre spoke of women as if he was at a horse fair.

'Then you are mistaken, sir,' Yves replied. 'My mind was on the competition, not a lady but, I grant you, she is fine. Who is she?'

'Sylvie St Berthaud, my lord.'

De Barre's eyes narrowed. He would play along with Sainton's game, for a while.

'Tell me about her,' Yves commanded arrogantly.

'She is an orphan and the ward of your rival, Jean Aubade, who, may I remind you, is favourite with Monsieur le Duc at the moment.'

He stared at Sylvie, who was chattering excitedly with the gossip of a portrait painter, Elise Baptiste.

'She is both spirited and talented at sculpture, a profession hardly becoming a young woman, but she is stubborn. She would be better served looking for a wealthy husband.'

De Barre was watching for any change of expression in Sainton's face, but it remained impassive.

'You seem to know a lot about her. Tell me more,' he said.

'I know a great deal about most things that happen here, my lord marquis,' de Barre replied suavely. 'But, in the girl's case, I was acquainted with her parents. Such a pity!'

Yves lifted his eyebrows again and de Barre

continued.

'Her father, Leon, was a traitor.'

'Harsh words, sir!'

'He defied the King in the matter of the Succession, and I exposed his treachery. At that time, Sylvie was a babe in arms, whose mother, Victoire, had died from fever after the birth. Afterwards, St Berthaud fled with the child to Chantilly, where he had his estates.'

'And you were recompensed for doing your duty to France?'

'I received the estates on his demise! I will not say his death was unfortunate. May all such traitors perish!'

Then de Barre put on his most sombre face.

'But I felt some guilt regarding his orphaned daughter.'

'How noble of you, but, if St Berthaud was a traitor, why should you feel any responsibility.'

Yves' expression did not change, but his eyes were fixed steadfastly on de Barre's face.

'I am a good Catholic. I must forgive, and it was not the child's fault. She was left with no protector. If le Duc had not ordered the little wench to be placed with Aubade, her distant cousin, I would have taken her myself.'

'How touching,' Yves replied sincerely. 'I applaud your noble sentiments but had you done so, what would have been the consequences when she was grown and discovered your part in her tragic history?'

Drawing out his fine cambric handkerchief,

de Barre sniffed and dabbed his eyes as he stalked off without a reply.

* * *

Sylvie darted several covert glances across the short distance to where de Barre and his companion were engaged in deep conversation outside their tent. Yves Sainton looked such a dandy in his fashionable coat, waistcoat and breeches. How different he had appeared the night before, when unadorned. Today, he seemed a peacock like the rest of the chevaliers. But he was still more handsome than any gentleman present.

Beneath his fashionable attire, however, his stance was still a soldier's. He was wearing his sword, the weapon which had held her hat, but, this morning, its hilt was ornamented with a great brown velvet bow!

Although Sylvie's experience with men was sadly lacking, she could not fail to notice that the marquis's eyes had hardly left her since she had been handed down from her carriage. His frequent glances were disconcerting, not hot as they had been in the forest, nor pleading like the night before, but all-enveloping, as if he was appraising her worth, body and soul. And when that toad, de Barre, had joined him, he, too, had stared at her, as if she was a piece of horseflesh. So she had determined to ignore their rudeness, but it was easier said than done.

However, there were many other things to view. A dais had been erected, which looked like a stage. Sylvie had never attended a public theatre, but, now her dear Jean was destined to be as an actor, pointing out and explaining his ideas for the stables. She was eagerly waiting to hear his presentation like the rest of the company. The whole stage fluttered with pennons and banners, and standing to guard it were soldiers, stiffly erect.

The emblems of Italy, Germany and Spain fluttered lightly as did the lion of England but, privately, the English were believed to have no chance, given their phlegmatic outlook on Art and their stiff-necked attitude to all things French. But it was the group of tents adorned with the lily of France that Sylvie's eyes kept returning to.

She turned to Elise once more.

'When will we see Jean?'

If she had not been a woman, she could have been with him in his tent now, going over the presentation. She knew he was very nervous. When Elise had asked him if he was going to practise his speech in the tent, he had replied curtly.

'No. I did my work last night. I shall not look at what I have to say again, until I read it on the stage. Otherwise I shall be all mixed-up.'

Sylvie hoped he was going to be all right. He

looked so pale, but he had no need to worry. Monsieur le Duc had him as favourite and she had even heard some of the ladies making wagers through their servants on him winning. But Yves Sainton was second favourite.

'As Jean heads the French team, he will be the first of our men to speak,' Elise pronounced. 'Yves should follow. What a clever young man he is! And how handsome. Just keep your eyes on the herald over there, Sylvie. He will blow the trumpet for the beginning of the presentations.'

Sylvie thought that her praise for the marquis was, to say the least, indelicate, given her closeness to Jean's and Sylvie's own presence, but she had suspected from Elise's communication of his virtues that madame was well disposed towards Yves Sainton.

'Now, come, my dear, to our places, near the dais,' Elise added.

Sylvie followed madame and the others to the rows of gilt chairs placed in front of the stage. The seats were shielded on three sides with great white canvases to frustrate the wind, which was blowing stronger now. Once they were seated, Sylvie could breathe easily again. She had lost sight of the marquis, but not for long.

Suddenly, he was bowing low before them. Sylvie could hardly bear it. What if he let slip they had already made each other's acquaintance?

'My lord!' Elise said, then she turned to Sylvie. 'May I introduce Mam'selle Sylvie St Berthaud, whom I have the pleasure of chaperoning. Sylvie, this is the Marquis of Sainton.'

Sylvie sat stiffly, although she was blushing. She held out her gloved hand, which he took for a moment, pressing his lips against it. She could feel the heat through the fabric.

'Mam'selle, what a pleasure. But, surely we have met before.'

Sylvie held her breath. Was he going to reveal their meeting?

'Surely not, my lord,' Elise cried. 'Sylvie has only just come to Court on the personal invitation of Monsieur le Duc. She is an accomplished sculptress, working in marble on a grand tableau. She is here, like me, to witness her cousin's presentation.'

'Her cousin?'

'Monsieur Jean Aubade!'

'Ah!'

Yves' eyebrows rose as if he had never heard of Jean. Sylvie felt sick at his pretence, which was as convincing as the most accomplished of actors.

'Our rival, madame?'

'Yes, but also a Frenchman,' Elise reminded him, smiling. 'May the best man win, as long as it is one of our countrymen. And how is your dear maman?'

'Very well, when I last saw her. I intend to

visit her when I return to Versailles.'

Sylvie noted that his arrogant tone changed to a softer one when he spoke of his mother.

'And will that be soon?'

'When His Majesty commands.'

'Then when you do, I beg you to convey my regards. And was His Majesty well when you were last together?'

As they engaged in the usual pleasantries, Sylvie sat silently.

'You are very quiet, Sylvie,' Elise reproved, turning to Yves challengingly. 'Well, what do you think of our newest addition to the Court then, my lord?'

'I have not seen such beauty, even in Versailles, madame,' Yves replied truthfully. 'It quite disarms me.'

He had his hand on his sword hilt.

'Oh, sir, you flatter dear Sylvie. Be careful, my dear. Yves is well known for his conquests of pretty women,' Elise teased, her eyes sparkling merrily.

'Madame, you do me a disservice,' he countered, his eyes fixed fast on Sylvie's face. 'I am as constant as the moon.'

Several ladies nearby laughed at what Sylvie had hoped was a private conversation.

'So, mam'selle, you are a sculptress. I envy you. I cannot work in marble, only draw plans, which you will see very soon. And I have such plans.'

Sylvie's mouth went dry. He was far too

clever for his own good, repeating the words she had heard him utter the night before, taunting her with their meeting. He continued.

'What does your tableau represent, mam'selle? Classic mythology?'

Sylvie bristled as Elise interposed.

'I am sure Sylvie won't mind me saying she is working on a pair of the finest horses, modelled on the Greek, I believe.'

Yves looked astonished. Sylvie thought his present humour akin to pure wickedness!

'I beg you, madame, give me leave to visit mam'selle in her studio. I would love to see this tableau for myself.'

'But that would be wonderful, my lord. Sylvie would be overjoyed, I'm sure. Wouldn't you, dear?'

Sylvie nodded, then added tartly, 'Of course, but I have little time to waste, given the weight of the task.'

There was a gasp from several of the ladies. Yves' lips curved slowly into that maddening smile.

'Then, mam'selle, we will find time to be together. And, now,' he said, looking at the dais where the competitors were gathering, 'I must make haste to my seat. Au revoir, mesdames.'

He swept into a low bow and, next moment, he was strutting off in the direction of the stage, followed by his servant. Sylvie's eyes flashed.

'What mighty arrogance!' she gasped.

'Shh, Sylvie,' Elise warned, 'you must not offend the gentleman. He has great friends at Court.'

'Like de Barre,' Sylvie said, who appeared at that moment with le Duc and began to take his seat.

'Yes. Yves could be a powerful enemy,' Elise added, misunderstanding. 'And a wonderful lover.'

Sylvie glanced at her quickly.

'Any one of those ladies in front of us would have been too willing to take him up on his invitation. I think you have to. It will be good for you and Jean. Oh, dear, there he goes. He does look pale.'

Next moment, Sylvie and Elise were listening attentively to the first presentation but, time and time again, Sylvie found her eyes drawn to the nonchalant and careless attitude of the most handsome of all competitors, who sat there on the dais looking bored, as if he cared little about winning, or anything much at all.

The Germans had some good ideas. But, privately, Sylvie thought Jean had nothing to fear from them. She liked the plans outlined by the swarthy men from Spain, who glowered at their rivals seated on the dais and threw their hands about with expressive gestures. The tiny Italian competitor's hand and body gestures were even more ridiculous! Like Jean had said, he was full of cherubs and twirls. The Englishman followed. He was tall, broad and fair. His French accent was terrible and his plans restrained.

Sylvie was sure he would not win on account of his austerity and, finally, by the time the French were ordered to be ready, she felt in her heart that Jean's classical designs, with his sweep of arched windows and domed ceilings, must take precedence with Monsieur le Duc.

When her cousin stood up at the great lectern, looking sober and distinguished in grey silk coat and breeches, she was full of pride. His servant opened his bag and handed him—nothing! Silence fell over the whole company as they waited. Elise and Sylvie remained in agony. Jean's face was wretched and he looked near fainting. Then a herald-at-arms strode forward.

'The first of the French competitors, Monsieur Jean Aubade, cannot proceed with his presentation!' he announced.

A buzz rose through the audience and the wind blew the idle chattering away. Then, with a dark and serious look, Monsieur le Duc stood up and called for silence.

'As Monsieur Aubade cannot proceed, I call on the next of our competitors, Yves, Marquis of Sainton!'

He sat down again and the hum ceased and changed to frenzied applause as the handsome figure strode forward, followed by his servant.

Sylvie closed her eyes in agony, a thousand questions running wild in her brain. Was this the beginning of de Barre's treachery? Why had Jean been struck dumb? Yves Sainton was certainly not. His clear, measured tones rang out. Sylvie listened in a daze. When he finished, the ovation was tremendous. The courtiers were standing and his fellow contestants glowering. There was no doubt he would be in the final round.

But Sylvie's eyes were searching for Jean. She caught a glimpse of his frock coat disappearing towards his tent. Her heart ached for him and her anger mounted. If this was de Barre's work, she must find something to do to make him suffer. And if it was Sainton's, she would never forgive the man for hurting her dear cousin and herself so much! When all the presentations had been completed, Yves Sainton was pronounced the leader.

When they were leaving the dais, Sylvie had been the recipient of a triumphant look from de Barre, which was not softened by an almost sympathetic one from Yves. She could not believe he was sorry they had failed, and that he had not had some hand in Jean's fall from grace. As she and Elise commiserated with Jean, she could see that Elise was better at it than she and far less emotional.

'I had my plans with me in the tent. I never let my bags be touched, by anyone,' Jean repeated over and over again.

'When did you last see the plans?' Elise demanded.

'Last night. I told you, when I went through them, and I checked they were there, before we set off in the carriage.'

'And did you leave your bags anywhere?' Elise persisted.

The questions continued endlessly, but the outcome was the same. Madame expressed some hope that Monsieur le Duc would summon Jean later to give a private presentation. Then Jean admitted it would take him time to prepare the plans again. They were in his head, and the lost copies were the only ones he had committed to parchment. He was in despair. He had to find them.

Sylvie felt a true sense of desolation as she wandered aimlessly around outside the tent, watching the servants packing up. She felt especially responsible for the mishap. Then she saw de Barre, gloating, standing outside his own tent. She hesitated, then rashly followed him as he turned on his heel and disappeared inside his tent. She was very angry, and thoughtless.

'Well, Sylvie, have you taken my advice at last and come to your senses?' he asked.

'No, de Barre. I have come to repeat, you are a monster,' she accused. 'You were responsible for what happened to Jean, weren't you?'

'I could have been,' he said glibly. 'I did

warn you that things would go wrong, if you continued to refuse me.'

'Give me Jean's plans!' she cried.

De Barre got up and approached her.

'I don't have them,' he replied, 'but I may know where they are. And you can have them, if you are able to satisfy me.'

'Don't touch me,' Sylvie said.

The little voice in her head was reproving her for being so hasty. She was in a vulnerable position.

'I will report your treachery to Monsieur le Duc,' she added.

'Do you think he would believe you, a mere girl, who visits my tent, unchaperoned? Besides, he is particularly out of sorts with Jean at the moment. He had great hopes of his success and would not wish anyone other than a Frenchman to succeed.'

They faced each other.

'But there is another one, isn't there?' Sylvie challenged, bitterly. 'Your pet, Sainton. He managed very well.'

'You insult dear Yves? I thought you were fond of him.'

'What do you mean?'

Sylvie was taken aback.

'You know very well what I mean,' de Barre snarled, thrusting his face into hers. 'I saw you two together, last night!'

Sylvie's face went white.

'It hurt me. He accompanied you to your

chamber after the chase!'

'No,' Sylvie cried, but de Barre ignored her.

'I wonder what le Duc would think of such behaviour, or your precious Jean, or Elise Baptiste? You're a clever little minx, outwitting them. But you cannot outwit me. I know you, Sylvie. Remember, I have always known you. You were always a witch. You have ensnared me for years with your spells, and that pretty body. By God, I desire you!' he snarled. 'And I'll have you. Sainton will never possess you. We are all alone, Sylvie. Now give me what I want most in the world, and I will return Jean's plans.'

'No!'

She turned to run, but he caught her round the waist. She was realising with growing horror that he would not give up, that, this time, he intended to have his pleasure. She almost fainted as she felt his lips upon her neck. She fought against him. He was crushing himself against her. He was not a big man, but he was strong. She struggled madly. She must bargain with him. She might still outwit him.

'I beg you. I'll do as you say, but, please, please, not here.'

Mercifully, he stopped, and his ugly mouth was gashed with an evil smile as she panted, her eyes half-closed, too weak to run, bargaining for a breathing space.

'When? When?' he snarled.

'When what?' another voice said.

As Yves strode in, his keen eyes noted the situation.

'What's going on here?'

His eyes were as hard as his tone. Sylvie felt sick to the bottom of her stomach.

'Things got a little heated.'

De Barre was smiling and smoothing down his cravat.

'For some wild reason, the lady accused me of being involved with that charade outside, over Aubade's plans. When you came in, I was asking her when we could meet again to discuss it. As I told you, Mam'selle St Berthaud is volatile and highly strung.'

The lies went on and on. Yves was looking hard at her.

'Well, mam'selle, this is a pretty pickle. I find you here with Guy alone and near distraught. Where is Madame Elise?'

'With my cousin, in his tent. And he is lying,' she said. 'He . . .'

Then she stopped, remembering de Barre's threats, her precarious position and the need to recover Jean's precious plans.

'It is true I came here to question him, yes, even that I accused him. But he treated me very ill.'

Sylvie shivered to her very bones.

'And why should you think Monsieur de Barre had anything to do with your cousin's unhappy position?'

'Because he is so against him.'

Yves lifted his eyebrows and, staring hard at de Barre, questioned, 'Are you against this young woman and her cousin, sir?'

'I am not. I have always been her champion,' Guy said, his eyes regarding Sylvie.

'Well,' Yves replied, 'I cannot make much of this.'

She knew by his eyes that he thought she had been most unwise to come to de Barre's tent alone. He offered his hand.

'Come, mam'selle.'

De Barre looked about to follow, but stopped at Yves' warning glance.

'We will get to the bottom of this matter.'

She took his hand, feeling its safe warmth.

'Where are you taking me?' she asked weakly.

'Back to your friends.'

'I hope I am still your friend, Sylvie,' de Barre said smoothly.

He had recovered his composure, but she did not answer.

'And that you will find Jean's plans,' he went on. 'If I should happen upon them, I will return them safely to you personally.'

She knew what the threat meant. She kept silence, still clinging on to the marquis' hand for support. Once outside, she saw his carriage.

'I cannot go with you in that, sir. I must return to Jean's tent. He and Elise will be wondering what has happened to me.'

'Then we will find them together, but not before you and I have had words.'

'What do you mean?'

He was still holding her hand, looking hard at her, his eyes searching her face as if he desired to hear the truth from her lips.

'I have nothing to say to you.'

She wanted to add she was grateful for her rescue, but the words wouldn't come out.

'You are stubborn, Sylvie, just as when you galloped away from me in the forest. What would have happened to you if I had not interposed?'

Her cheeks flamed at his question and her own thoughts.

'Why were you so indiscreet to visit a gentleman in his tent?'

'I cannot tell you,' Sylvie cried, 'but it was all de Barre's fault. You have no right to question me.'

'As your deliverer, I have every right,' he said, looking down at her, his heart aching at her plight.

He let go her hand.

'I told you, things are different at Court. Men have great desires, and little will stop them, once their minds are made up to it.'

Small, wet tendrils of hair clung to her forehead and her lashes were wet. Her clothes were in disarray. Earlier on, wearing the green and white gown had given her the guise of an elegant lily. Now, the satin was rumpled and his quick eyes took in a tear, where the bodice lacing had ripped awry.

'You are far too tempting, mam'selle,' he said, adding, 'Visiting any man's tent alone would be bound to bring disaster.'

'Only if that man was a brute,' Sylvie replied.

In spite of bridling at his reproof, she felt an annoyingly delicious throb inside at his words.

'I do not desire your two-handed compliments, sir. I only want to return to my cousin and Madame Baptiste. You may think it wise to reprove me, but I had my reasons for visiting de Barre alone. I will not be misunderstood on that count. And rash though it may have seemed, I was truly grateful for your intervention.'

It took a lot for her to say it.

'Then I am satisfied that I have been able to do you some good service for once.'

His face brightened.

'Now, what about the missing plans? Let me escort you to your cousin and Madame Baptiste. Perhaps I can be of help in recovering them.'

She looked into his eyes, which seemed honest and full of sympathy. This man was a veritable chameleon, who could change his colours at will.

'I doubt it, sir,' she said.

Whatever he had done for her, she could hardly trust him, yet. That little warning voice was telling her to go carefully. Indeed, Yves Sainton himself might have been the agent of her cousin's downfall!

CHAPTER FIVE

Sylvie, what happened?' Elise cried. 'Where have you been? I was about to send out a searching party. What does this mean, my lord?'

Sylvie held her breath as Yves shot her a quick glance from under his fine brows and, taking out his handkerchief, sniffed delicately.

'I found your charge in a distressed position a distance away.'

Would he give away her indiscretion to Elise and her cousin? Then in one glorious moment of relief, she heard him add, 'But, all is well, madame. Unfortunately, she had tripped and fallen.'

'Fallen? How?'

'I believe upon the ropes of a tent. At the same time as she was unfortunate enough to damage her gown, I was fortunate enough to be passing.'

Elise broke away and, picking up a light cloak, swathed Sylvie in it.

Elise's eyes regarded the two of them keenly.

'Sylvie? Is this true?'

She nodded shamefacedly.

'I'm so sorry, Elise. I shouldn't have gone off like that. This awful hoop tripped me. I'm afraid I've ruined the gown. I suppose I was upset about Jean losing the plans and was not looking where I was going.'

Would Elise swallow the lame excuse? Evidently so, because she was smiling at the marquis with a relieved look on her face.

'Then we have you to thank, my lord,' she said. 'We wouldn't want Sylvie coming to any harm, would we, Jean?'

Her cousin, still pale-faced from his humiliation, started at Elise's words and came forward. Then, extending his hand, he kissed Yves briefly on both cheeks.

'Yes, my lord, we have you to thank, twice.'

Sylvie looked up at him astonished.

'Twice?' she echoed.

'For saving you, and for restoring the honour of France.'

Yves frowned a little.

'With your presentation, my lord. At least you did not let the side down, like me!'

Jean shook his head and, turning, sat down on a stool, dropping his head into his hands. Sylvie had never seen him so depressed, except when Nadine died. Yves regarded both of them.

'I am sorry to see you distressed, Monsieur Aubade. I warrant that had you taken your opportunity, sir, my designs would have come out worse.'

For a man of such an arrogant nature, his humble tone and generous words were something of a revelation. Sylvie asked herself for the hundredth time, could this sincere young man really be a rogue?

'May I help to recover your spirits in any way?' he added.

'I wish you could, sir, but I think my designs must have been stolen by some jealous rival, otherwise where would they be?'

He shrugged his shoulders miserably.

'It is not only the plans. Worse, indeed, when companion artists turn into felons and betray the good name of Art.'

'I agree,' Yves replied, his eyes flashing.

If only Sylvie could trust him. She dearly wanted to. His present expressions of regret and his offer to help them, coupled with her own rescue and the fiery enthusiasm she had seen when he made his earlier speech, seemed to indicate Yves Sainton was not their enemy. But then she remembered that he was a rival and the ally of de Barre!

'What could you do to help us, sir?' she asked, hugging the cloak around her.

'I will instigate a thorough search. I will question certain people in high office, which your cousin might find difficult to do.'

She was sure he meant de Barre.

'I will also speak with Monsieur le Duc. Hopefully, he can be persuaded on a private audience so Jean will not lose his chance. I know he values your cousin's work a great deal. I may have presented plans of my own, but I do not condone such treachery on a fellow artist.'

Sylvie flushed at the reproach.

'Of course, we do not think ill of you, my lord. Sylvie meant no harm,' Elise interposed.

'Then, sir, I would be very grateful.'

There was hope in Jean's eyes as he offered his hand, which Yves took.

'Cheer yourself, sir. France will be the better for it. Now I must hasten to my carriage, which I would be delighted to share with you. I assume your own means of conveyance has departed.'

He raised his eyebrows.

'Thank you, my lord,' Jean said. 'We would be happy to take advantage of that offer, too.'

Elise was nodding in agreement. Sylvie's heart raced. Her own position was becoming increasingly difficult. She possessed the knowledge of who had done them wrong, but was unable to disclose it.

A few moments later, Yves was handing her into his fashionable barouche and she was pulling her cloak about her. The proximity of Yves Sainton both bewitched and confused her. The marquis spent his time making gallant conversation with her and her companions as well as taking the opportunity to closely scrutinise her person. To her discomfort, she could not take her eyes off him either. And there was no way to avoid his glances, except dropping one's eyes in the way of a coquette, which appeared to make him worse.

Jean did not seem to notice the by-play. He was too wrapped up in his own thoughts. Strangely, neither did Elise, although she appeared to be intent on every word the marquis spoke. Finally, when they arrived outside the chateau and were handed down by the servants, he doffed his hat.

'I hope to see you all later at dinner in the Grand Salon. There will be both music and dancing to accompany our meal. I am sure Mam'selle Sylvie will enjoy that.'

His lips were curving into that mocking smile again, which she had not seen for some time, given the serious disposition of the last few hours.

'I'm sure she will, my lord,' Elise replied, answering for her.

'And I hope that I may mark her dancing card. May I have the pleasure of dancing with you, Sylvie?'

'If you please, my lord,' she replied.

She had only danced the minuet in her dreams, or in the privacy of her own bedroom. But, with him? The thought made the heat rise in her face.

'Au revoir, mesdames Aubade.'

Jean inclined his head and, with a final

flourish of his hat, Yves turned on his heel. They watched his retreat for a moment then Elise squeezed Sylvie's arm.

'Isn't he wonderful?' she enthused.

Sylvie glanced at Jean, wondering how he would take madame's enthusiasm towards his rival but, once again, he was preoccupied.

'And you like him, Sylvie, I can see,' Elise added, whispering, 'This has been a most unfortunate day for your cousin, but I can see his and your own fortunes are changing.'

Then she raised her voice.

'Sylvie, my dear, I believe you have made a conquest. Imagine! The Marquis of Sainton! What girl could be more fortunate than to have gained such avid interest from a noble young chevalier, who is prime favourite with young King Louis! Mark my words, you will be receiving an invitation to Versailles in the very near future, if I know anything about it.'

Elise smiled in a satisfied manner and, taking Jean's arm, she indicated Sylvie should take his other.

'Now, cheer yourselves, both of you. Jean, are you listening? I'm sure your lost designs will be discovered and that Monsieur le Duc will be merciful. Sylvie?'

'Yes, madame?'

'We must think about what you are going to wear this evening. I will call in my own dressmaker for advice. Something tasteful, but outstanding. You must sparkle tonight. We women artists must show that we are a match for the men.'

Privately, Sylvie wondered when she would ever get more of her marble horses done, having lost several days' labour already, but the prospect of the evening thrilled her, in spite of her fear of further confrontation with de Barre. At least he could do her no harm in company.

That evening, Sylvie could see Yves Sainton and Guy de Barre sitting next to each other at the highest table, in the place of importance, on the right hand of Monsieur le Duc, who was evidently not in the best of humours.

It was rumoured he was disappointed at the length of time it was taking to choose who was to design his stables and, in fact, Sylvie had just heard someone remark that he would have preferred being with his horses than preside over a fine banquet. Monsieur was dark-skinned and had chosen a coat of gold brocade, ornamented with a fine, lace cravat, which reached almost to his waist. He was of sturdy build and wore a luxurious, curling wig, which flowed over his stocky shoulders.

She could not see the rest of him, but she knew his legs were bowed from constant riding. He had a way with horses like no-one else, and Sylvie was sure le Duc would admire her tableau, when the time came to show it! Her thoughts and gaze returned to Yves Sainton. That evening he cut a fine figure, resplendent in a russet red frock coat of the most elegant style, elaborately embellished with silver thread. De Barre, alongside, reminded Sylvie of the devil himself in his black.

She stared at Yves, trying to get the puzzle straight in her mind. He had rescued her twice already. She should be grateful but she still feared he had some devious motive. De Barre had not failed to notice her either because his lustful eyes returned again and again to her as she sat quietly beside Elise and Jean.

'Are you enjoying yourself, Sylvie?' Elise asked. 'See, Yves is in the place of honour, as befits his rank. Of course le Duc cherishes his importance as the King's favourite playmate and, as a member of the Regency Council, wishes to keep on the good side of him.'

Sylvie could see she was sporting. Elise never seemed at a loss for words as she gossiped on. Sylvie's eyes had been so dazzled by the array of food and the sumptuous table decorations that she had ventured to ask Madame Elise if she thought le Duc's table rivalled that of the King himself.

'Ah, no, Sylvie,' Elise quipped merrily. 'There is absolutely no place like Versailles for food or quality of manners. It is breathtaking in its beauty and hopefully, you will see for yourself. Indeed, if Yves does not invite you, I will, when I have finished le Duc's portrait and I am recalled by the King.'

Sylvie was so wrapped up in Elise's interesting anecdotes about the King and his Court, that she did not notice the fair-haired page approaching to whisper something to her cousin. As the page retreated to the high table, Jean's face had brightened considerably.

'I have been asked to take a turn about with Sainton and le Duc, as soon as the company rises and the dancing begins,' he communicated excitedly.

'There, I told you so,' Elise replied.

'I'm so happy for you, Jean,' Sylvie said.

'It may not be good news. He may wish to discharge me and replace my designs with Sainton's. I don't know why I thought the man a fop when I first met him. He has a brilliant head on those broad shoulders, which contains a rare talent. I would like him as a fellow artist and a friend.'

Sylvie thought privately she would have liked it, too, if it had been remotely possible!

'I'm sure it will be good news,' Elise said. 'And I believe that Yves will have a hand in it. Remember, he said he would.'

Elise was looking directly at him now, and was rewarded with an enigmatic smile. Once again, Sylvie found herself wondering just how well Elise knew the marquis.

Soon she and Elise were seated with the other ladies, listening to the orchestra, and, while she sat, intent upon the music, Sylvie had become the recipient of the admiring glances of many gentlemen present, both young and old, who gathered around her. In her wonderful gown, she sparkled naturally as Elise had promised she would. Elise's dressmaker had done Sylvie proud. The gown was deep saffron, which accentuated the warm colour of her eyes, but they turned cold when she saw de Barre approaching. In his sombre black attire, he reminded her now of some ugly hobgoblin come to cast an ill spell on the company. She clutched her stiff dance card, hoping to hide it in her skirts. But it was too late!

'Good evening, ladies. May I join you?'

Next moment, he was taking her card and scrutinising it.

'You may, Monsieur de Barre. I trust you are well.'

Elise's voice had a sharp edge, but she knew better than to antagonise Monsieur le Duc's adviser.

'Very well, madame, and I hope to be even better after having the pleasure of dancing with Mam'selle St Berthaud.'

Sylvie shuddered at the thought. His mean eyes scanned the small card.

'Ah, so many dances free. I am grateful for my luck.'

'Those first are taken, monsieur,' she said, snatching it back. 'I have not set down the name yet.'

'By whom?'

'By the Marquis of Sainton!'

Sylvie saw Elise raise her eyebrows, but de Bare smiled suavely.

'He's a lucky young pup attempting to monopolise such beauty. But I will take the next dance, he is otherwise engaged with le Duc.'

Sylvie sat helplessly, hardly listening to the music, only praying for rescue.

The dances began without le Duc's presence and the first in the suite was led by his richly-dressed chief minister, who began the sequence by circling around the glittering room. When de Barre took her hand and led her forward, Sylvie was sick with disgust at the slight brush of his body against her, and his cold, wet hand in hers. Unfortunately, the suite was composed of several dances, which were continuous. Did her loathing show on her face? She realised that there were many envious eyes watching her progress, as she danced with a man whose influence with le Duc was most sought after. But she hated him.

As they circled, he insisted on whispering bold compliments to her.

'You look wonderful, Sylvie. You are like a jewel, and I will set you in my crown. And you will come to me of your own accord.'

'I will never submit, monsieur,' she hissed back.

'Then Jean will pay,' he retorted, his eyes glittering. 'Think hard about what harm could be done to your dear cousin. I warned you of it in the forest. And I will carry it out. Just think what I can give you. All this!'

He indicated the company about him.

'Dancing every day, and jewels. All yours, Sylvie, if you will be mine.'

Several times as they passed Elise, Sylvie could see the sympathy in the woman's eyes, but she was unable to do anything to rescue her. Guy de Barre's eyes narrowed with pleasure at her growing discomfort. Sylvie shivered at the thought of his arms about her person. She hoped she was not going to be sick. She must leave the floor. As the music slowed again, ready to strike up the gavotte, she feigned a small cry of pain.

'Sylvie?' he said, his tone hard.

'My ankle, monsieur. It is weak. I must pass on the gavotte.'

'You witch.' He smiled. 'I think your real intention is to dance with me no more. But I will not force you.'

He gripped her arm and escorted her through the other dancers and off the floor. As they walked through the throng, with Sylvie feigning a slight limp, he hissed in her ear.

'The day will come when you dance with me in my bedchamber, Sylvie!'

She closed her eyes briefly, full of horror at the thought. She would rather kill herself. Then she almost cried out with relief. Jean, accompanied by Yves Sainton, was making his way through the company. As de Barre delivered her to her seat, Elise pressed her arm sympathetically. Jean had reached them! She was safe, for now.

'Well?' Elise asked.

Jean had a satisfied smile on his face, while Yves' expression seemed to tell Sylvie not to worry. But was his compassion real?

'You were right, madame,' Jean cried. 'Le Duc has offered me the chance to present my plans privately. They are safe and sound.'

'How?' Sylvie cried, darting a triumphant glance at de Barre, who was glowering evilly.

'I do not know how, but they were restored to me by the marquis. I cannot thank him enough.'

Yves was looking into Sylvie's face. She could see he was searching for some expression of gratitude from her.

'Nor I,' she said, lifting her chin.

Of course, he had every opportunity to restore them, but what was his motive in doing so? Yves bowed low. De Barre was very close to her and she shrank from him.

'Good news, Aubade!'

De Barre's congratulations were sickening.

'Perhaps you will take more care to protect your designs now. There are men about who wish you ill, given your favour with le Duc. I congratulate you on succeeding with a private audience, but you have much ground to make up after the success of our friend here.'

Yves inclined his head,

'I am most indebted to the marquis,' Jean replied. 'And his designs are worthy of much praise.'

He was looking at Sylvie's flushed face.

'Have you been dancing, my dear? Good. I think we can all enjoy ourselves a little now.'

Suddenly, he offered his arm to Elise.

'Shall we, madame?'

Was Sylvie to be left alone with de Barre? But, this time, a saviour presented himself. Yves was bowing.

'Shall we?' he repeated, offering his arm.

De Barre's eyes glinted.

'Be careful of mam'selle's ankle, Yves. She strained it dancing with me!'

With these sarcastic words, he strode away.

'Can your ankle stand if, Sylvie?' Yves asked, darting a mischievous glance at her.

'I feel somewhat better now, my lord,' Sylvie replied truthfully.

'Good.'

Next moment, the marquis was leading Sylvie forward and she was suddenly conscious of many pairs of eyes fixed upon them once more, as they joined Jean and Elise upon the floor. As Sylvie turned on Yves' arm, his closeness was overwhelming. His lithe body was in perfect tune with hers as they turned in time with the music, and the strong grasp of his fingers, as he led her in the intricate steps, made her head dizzy.

She felt his hand tighten in hers and her cheeks go hot. Consciously she did not wish to flirt with him, but she vas powerless to resist, faced with such overwhelming attraction.

'Do you know the origin of this allemande, Sylvie?' he asked, as they came together again.

She could not trust herself to answer, knowing that her close scrutiny of him had evoked the question.

'The dance came out of Germany, where good Protestants called it indecent. They say it leads to love-making, Sylvie.'

Yves realised with the instinctive knowledge of his maleness, that, in spite of his lovely partner's outward mistrust of his motives, her instant reciprocation of his touch showed that in the game of love she would consume a man with her flaring passion.

'You are silent. Did my words offend your sensibilities?'

He was looking at her quizzically, as they were close together once more.

'Not your words,' she answered, staring into his eyes.

'But?'

'But your true motives.'

Sylvie was playing his game also, or was she merely fishing for pretty compliments?'

'What else could a man think of but love-making confronted with such beauty,' he quipped but Yves was both surprised and dismayed to see the glint of tears in those lovely eyes.

He cursed himself for being so churlish.

'You talk of love,' she said. 'I have known precious little.'

The music was slowing now.

'Forgive my careless words then, mam'selle,' he replied courteously.

They were only a breath apart. He glanced across at Jean and Elise.

'Your cousin loves you for sure, as does madame. They continually look for your welfare.'

Her eyes searched his handsome face, wanting the truth and not finding it. But even the lack of explanation could not overcome the magnetic sense she felt as she was drawn to him. Suddenly, the orchestra began to strike up the minuet, which Sylvie felt was the most beautiful of dances.

'The minuet,' he said. 'I claim my dance, mam'selle!'

He could not wait to feel her touch again. Sylvie stretched out her hand for his and lifted her skirts delicately with the other. It was the culmination of the suite, a measure that a girl danced with the man of her dreams. He was bowing ceremoniously, his dark eyes probing hers, and she was curtseying. With her hand in his, they glided forward as one, their feet measuring out the complicated steps, their minds only on each other. As he drew her to the right, then the left, he felt her threading into his soul. They were weaving a bond, as if they were the only man and woman on earth.

This was the dance of courtship, searching for the soul's mate, retreating, joining together, side by side, facing full on, then gliding past and beginning all over again.

'Mam'selle,' he said as the dance slowed finally, 'your dancing is exquisite.'

Sylvie came to at his words, the spell broken. If only the moment could have lasted, if only he was sincere.

'Have I offended you?' he repeated, searching her face, trying to divine its expression.

'No, my lord.'

She had returned to reality, and pressed her lips together in pure disappointment. Across the room, she could see de Barre, standing with one of Jean's rivals, an ugly look on his face. How long had he been watching her dancing with Yves? She shuddered and passed a small hand over her heated brow as the marquis escorted her to her seat.

As she sat down, Yves bowed and said, 'Mam'selle Sylvie's skill in the minuet would enchant the King himself. Let us hope that, soon, she may grace the dancing floor at Versailles on his personal invitation.'

But the look on de Barre's face was absorbing her attention, and she failed to notice Elise signal a triumphant look from behind her ivory fan. Sylvie tossed her head back and set her chin like she had done when de Barre had assaulted her in the forest. She would show him by her fearless glance that she was not afraid. Then, to her dismay, she was conscious that Yves, who was standing beside her, had ceased his conversation with Elise, and had noticed the by-play between her and de Barre!

Sylvie burned with shame inside, thinking of how the marquis had also surprised them that morning in the tent. Suddenly, she realised that what she desired as much as Yves' truthfulness was his good opinion of her. She could not bear it if he believed there was some intimacy between her and Guy de Barre.

De Barre had turned to the swarthy man beside him.

'I can see you are not happy, Don Morales, also that you were studying the marquis' dancing prowess. Is it not as good as his architecture?'

The question was meant to stir up trouble.

'The devil take him! The young fop is too accomplished for his own good. His presentation was almost perfect.'

'He is such a close friend of your young king that, personally, I believe he is bound to triumph. And, of course, he is a Frenchman,' de Barre replied cunningly.

He knew the Spaniard's jealous mind only too well, and their patriotic causes ran parallel.

The present King of Spain was a

Frenchman. Charles II of Spain had no heir of his own and had willed that the teenage Philip should be king when he died, but must swear never to be King of France as well. So, at seventeen years old, on the death of Charles, Philip had been set on the Spanish throne. But many Spaniards had no wish to see a foreigner rule their country, and Don Morales was one of them.

De Barre had always been a sympathiser with that Spanish cause. It was his dearest wish to see young King Louis deposed, and Philip in his rightful place. He had more claim to the throne of France. From his own time at Versailles, de Barre knew that if the old King had known that all his immediate heirs would die of smallpox, he would never have allowed his true surviving heir, his grandson, Philip, to sign away his rights to France.

But he had, at the Treaty of Utrecht, and de Barre saw there was only one solution. If the boy king met with an accident, then the way would be open for Philip's return to France. And Yves Sainton was the means to young Louis' side. This was de Barre's greatest desire, to rid himself of the King and second, to claim Sylvie as his own, willing or unwilling.

'I understand that Sainton will be returning to Versailles very soon on the orders of the King,' he added suavely. 'It can be a dangerous expedition through the forest.'

The inference was extremely clear.

'And when will this journey take place?' the Spaniard asked with a murderous glance.

'I do not know the day or the hour yet,' de Barre replied, 'but soon I will. However if I am able to communicate such sensitive information, I will expect some return.'

Don Morales lifted an eyebrow. Le Duc's adviser was a wily old fox, but both his country and himself stood to profit from de Barre's cunning.

'Go on.'

'That girl,' de Barre whispered, indicating Sylvie, as Yves escorted her from the dance floor.

Don Morales smiled. Until now, he had thought the man was a cold fish.

'I desire her and I mean to take her. And I have it on the best authority that she will be travelling with him. If I furnish you with Sainton's movements, you must kidnap the girl and bring her to a place of my choosing. She is not to be harmed, nor touched in any way. She's mine. It is up to you what you do with Sainton, but his loss would plunge His Majesty into the greatest depression. I have heard the boy is not in the best of health.'

Don Morales' eyes glinted. There was nothing he wanted more than to cause harm to the boy King and also rid himself of his greatest rival in the competition. He neither knew or cared who had dispatched the previous French favourite, Jean Aubade, but he suspected it was the Italians, whom he hated just as much.

After making their arrangements, the Spaniard bowed briefly then left de Barre, pleased with his plotting. Stealing Aubade's plans and setting the competitors at each others' throats was working most satisfactorily. Guy de Barre was confident that Yves, who was his passport to the King, would escape unscathed. Then all he had to hope was that fate would be with him. He needed more than luck in his attempt to kidnap Sylvie.

CHAPTER SIX

Sylvie stood back and surveyed her marble horses critically. She had ordered one of their servants to place the ladders against the scaffolding, in a position where she could continue the fine work upon the horses' curling manes with the flat chisel she was holding.

She was swathed in her working apparel, a jacket, fastened with hooks and eyes and a cream-coloured petticoat dress. Her simple clothes gave her the appearance of a servant girl rather than a young lady of quality. She had tucked her auburn locks under a mob cap, which was tied with ribbon under her chin. She was ready for work and not for visitors.

'Sylvie, they're magnificent!' Elise cried, who had been watching the unveiling.

'You think so?'

'I know a real artist when I see one,' Elise complimented. 'You have managed such wonderful lines, so delicate but strong as well.'

Sylvie thrilled with pride.

'Did you use a model?'

'Poor old Pelotte.'

Both laughed merrily. There was nothing in Sylvie's fine tableau to suggest a sign of the dear old piebald. Sylvie hitched up her skirts farther and set her foot on the ladder. Soon, she was standing high up on the platform.

'Be careful, dear,' Elise called as she seated herself below and began to sketch from notes.

Then she began to prattle on about last night's dancing and, of course, the marquis.

'I am quite sure Yves will arrange an invitation to Versailles for you, Sylvie, and, perhaps, an audience with Louis himself. His Majesty is such a sweet-faced boy and has the most expressive eyes. I would dearly like to paint him in his ceremonial robes.'

While she was speaking, Sylvie concentrated on cutting through a streaked plane of marble and drawing out yet another delicate curl with her chisel. She was so wrapped up in her work that she did not notice Elise's hurried rise from her chair, nor her graceful curtsey to the small band of courtiers who had entered the studio quietly and were now watching Sylvie.

'Well, Yves,' le Duc murmured, 'Hercules' labours over the Aegean stables could not have been as seriously undertaken. What beauty!'

'I told you that the tableau was fine, monsieur,' Yves whispered.

'You have pointed out Mam'selle Berthaud's talents most certainly,' he quipped. 'Will you make her aware of our presence, Madame Baptiste? But, softly, I would not want her surprised at such a height.'

His eyes danced merrily.

'Sylvie,' Elise called. 'Sylvie! We have visitors!'

'Oh!'

She was quite shocked to see the small knot of gentlemen gazing up at her. She dared not curtsey in case she fell. Yves stared upwards and his warm gaze rested on her slight form, swathed in classic cream.

'Pardon,' she called, recognising le Duc. 'I'll be down directly.'

Next moment, Yves dismissed the approaching servant and took hold of the ladder himself. The gentlemen talked amongst themselves as Sylvie descended. Next moment, she was facing the elegant company, conscious of her simple dress and her dishevelled appearance.

'Well, mam'selle,' le Duc began, regarding her, 'the Marquis of Sainton has been raving to us about your talent and persuaded me to visit you at work. Isn't that right, Yves?'

'It is, monsieur! And was I not right? Isn't the tableau fine?'

'You were speaking the truth!' le Duc replied, staring up at the horses. 'When your work is completed, where would you like to see these noble animals placed?' he asked Sylvie finally.

The company was silent. Sylvie breathed in, determined to try her luck.

'I should like to see them adorning the gates of your grand stables, monsieur,' she replied decidedly.

'So you intend to have these beauties prancing over the gateway to my stables?'

Monsieur le Duc's eyes twinkled. Madame Elise interposed.

'Sylvie has great ambitions, monsieur. I hope you are not offended by her plain speaking.'

'I am not,' le Duc replied. 'I find plain speaking in any lady a novelty.'

The chevaliers tittered. Elise gave a small curtsey and exchanged glances with Sylvie.

'I think your horses are the most spirited of beasts, mam'selle,' le Duc went on. 'Indeed, they would grace the gates of Paradise.'

'Thank you, monsieur.'

'As for my stables,' he said, his eyes twinkling still, 'they are yet to be constructed and only will be when this young fellow stirs himself enough to finish his designs and allow me to employ the builders. Then, and only then, shall we make our decisions on their ornamentation.'

His head had turned to address his remark to Yves. Sylvie's elation at le Duc's interest in her work was suddenly deflated. Had he chosen the marquis over Jean after all? If he had, then de Barre's treachery had worked! Then Yves spoke.

'But there is one architect's designs still to be shown, monsieur, Jean Aubade, whom you've agreed to meet this very afternoon. I am sure you'll be pleasantly surprised with his plans for the stables, if his lady cousin's talent is anything to go by.'

Le Duc nodded as Yves defended Jean.

'Yes, I am well reminded what a talented family this lady comes from. You have grown into a lovely young woman, Sylvie,' he said. 'I am glad to see you back at Court.'

'Thank you, sir.'

'But not for long.'

Sylvie stared with astonishment at the words.

'No, child, don't be afraid. Only for a short time. I am sending you to Versailles.'

Elise suppressed a cry of delight.

'It is for your own good.'

'But what about helping Jean? And I haven't finished my horses.'

Elise looked worried, but le Duc was smiling.

'Don't worry about your cousin, mam'selle. Aubade will find another willing helpmate. As for your horses, they will not break out from their marble, although they threaten to. You will see plenty of fine animals in His Majesty's stables, as well as statues of them by the greatest masters. Versailles is a wonderful treasure trove for Art and young artists.'

'Thank you, monsieur,' she said enthusiastically.

'Don't thank me, my dear, but Yves here. He was insistent that you should accompany him.'

Sylvie felt a delicious little thrill inside.

'It seems he has an undeniable hankering for a beautiful companion. We shall miss him, as well as Madame Baptiste.'

It was Elise's turn to look astonished.

'Yes,' le Duc went on, 'young Louis has recalled you, too, madame.'

Elise dropped a deep curtsey as she replied.

'I am at your service, monsieur. I will prepare myself at once.'

'Now, I must proceed with my rounds. I have one hundred live horses and twice as many hounds to inspect this morning! Once more, my compliments, Sylvie, upon your beasts. I have not seen a finer pair worked in marble for some years.'

He turned to Yves and lifted his thick eyebrows.

'I will leave you to your arrangements with

the ladies, Sainton.'

Then, with a meaningful glance at Yves, he bowed once more and turned, with the small company of gentlemen close at his heels. Yves remained.

'What wonderful news!' Elise cried. 'When do you intend to set out, my lord marquis?'

'I will inform you of that later, madame, but it will be soon.'

'Wonderful,' Elise enthused. 'Are you coming, Sylvie?'

'I'm afraid I'm not ready yet.'

She couldn't leave everything topsy-turvy. Elise nodded.

'Don't be too long then. There is a great deal for us both to do. Clothes and . . .' She rolled her eyes to heaven. 'And what are your present intentions, my lord?'

Yves lifted his eyebrows.

'Hopefully, to communicate the manner of the King's invitation to mam'selle.'

To Sylvie's great surprise and sudden relief, Elise did not offer to stay, and the thought of being alone with the marquis once more made Sylvie's pulse race. She felt extremely hot, so she took off the mob cap and shook her hair down over her shoulders. Sylvie looked up at him.

'Then I have you to thank for the invitation to Versailles, my lord?'

'You are looking forward to it?' he asked, inclining his head.

'Extremely,' she replied truthfully, 'but I am worried about Jean.'

'Why?'

'Because of leaving him.'

Her voice faltered a little. She could hardly accuse him of complicity in Jean's demise, in case it was unjust.

'And?' he probed.

'I am afraid something might happen, that someone will do him some harm. He has already lost his designs once!'

'And found them again,' Yves reminded her.

'Where were they?' she asked.

'They were delivered to me by one of de Barre's men.'

'Ah,' she said.

'I take it then that you knew that Guy de Barre had some knowledge of their disappearance.'

She realised that he was being as careful as she was, not to reveal himself. Sylvie felt the desperate urge to blurt out that de Barre was blackmailing her most foully. She felt both her virtue and her honesty were being questioned and, worst of all, she was being most dreadfully misunderstood which, for Sylvie, was suddenly quite heartbreaking.

'You remain silent, mam'selle.'

Once again, he was reminded of the fragile golden beauty of the tiger lily or some slim pale bloom, whose beautiful head held the weight of rain on its blossom and drooped accordingly.

'I know that de Barre means harm to Jean, my lord! But I cannot tell you why! I beg you, do not press me on the matter.'

'We are all entitled to our secrets, but take heart, Jean will be more circumspect after this,' he said seriously.

'I assume that you, too, have your secrets!' she said to cover herself.

'Too many,' he said. 'And, now, let us talk of more pleasant matters. When I informed His Majesty, in my last letter, that I had met a beautiful and talented young sculptress working for le Duc, he replied as I thought he would, that I should bring you to Versailles. The King has no wish that Monsieur le Duc should entertain the best artists. He has much of his great-grandfather's nature, who made Versailles the haunt of the greatest artisans in Europe, hence his interest. Whether or not Louis will grant you an audience I cannot tell, but one thing I know for sure is that the eyes and ears of his Court will be fixed upon you as much as they are here!'

'What do you mean?'

'I mean, Sylvie, that when someone as enchanting as you arrives at a world-weary Court there are many powerful men who are swift to take advantage, by any means, and I would not like to see that happen.'

She knew by his keen look he was referring once again to de Barre's disgusting behaviour and undoubted treachery.

'I thought you wanted to talk of pleasant things. And I am not afraid of powerful men!'

It was a courageous response if not quite true! He looked down at her quizzically, and felt desire rise in him once more.

'And here is one who wishes you no harm,' he said softly, getting himself under control.

Next moment, he was taking her hand and raising it to his lips. Immediately, her head was filled with the most impossible and delightful thoughts.

'I am glad of that, my lord,' she said clearly, withdrawing her hand.

Suddenly, she became aware of the power she exerted as a woman. De Barre had blamed her for driving him mad, and called her a witch and an enchantress. But his desires were evil and she could never reciprocate such lust. It was love, and only love, Sylvie would submit to with any man.

'And now,' she added coolly, 'I must get on. I have done so little today. How soon must I be ready to leave?'

'Within the next two days. It is a wearisome journey, and travelling through the forests can be dangerous,' he said.

It was her turn to arch her eyebrows. She was sure she knew the forests better than he did.

'I know everything about danger in the forest, if you remember,' she replied archly.

'Indeed, I could say that our first acquaintance did not lack that element!'

'And you will be as safe with me as you were then! You will travel comfortably with Madame Baptiste and keep her company in the carriage. I and my servants will ride alongside.'

She lifted her chin haughtily.

'Fie, sir,' she said carelessly. 'While I have my youth and strength, I intend to ride beside you. I have no desire to be cooped up in any carriage. Elise will have her maidservants to keep her company.'

He shrugged at such wilfulness. However, he had learned already Sylvie was as headstrong as she was beautiful, not accepting anyone's advice easily and certainly not his. So be it, Yves thought, admitting to himself he would not be sorry to have her as his travelling companion. But what mount would she use?

'Have you brought Pelotte with you?'

She was sorry after he had asked, but it was necessary. The old horse would never make it to Versailles.

'I have not, sir, but my cousin will furnish me with a suitable mount!'

Her eyes glinted dangerously.

'I am sure he will,' he said. 'The old horse was quite adequate for short distances but . . .'

'I know,' Sylvie snapped, curtailing the conversation.

She had no intention of letting him know

how he had wounded her feelings by mentioning Pelotte's inadequacies, or his hint that Jean would be unable to find her another mount. She finished tucking in her hair and was looking at the ladder as if she had the most urgent desire to be rid of him. He didn't reply, because a most pleasant thought had just occurred. He stared up at her tableau thoughtfully. Then he came back to himself.

'No, be assured, Sylvie, I was not mocking your piebald,' he said, 'but thinking you are worthy of a mount such as those you created.'

He indicated the marble horses. She looked at him sharply, searching for that mocking curl of the lips, but he seemed sincere.

'Thank you for the compliment, my lord,' she replied with a hint of sarcasm, 'but I do not think I will be lucky enough to gain such a mount. Now, sir,' she added decidedly, 'please call my servant over, so I can climb up again. I need to complete my horses' manes, before I can accompany you to Versailles.'

He smiled and complied, knowing that he was being dismissed. As he watched her climb up to the dais, he marvelled at her ability to overcome the hand of dubious cards fate had dealt her so far. But, hopefully, Sylvie's luck was about to change.

CHAPTER SEVEN

You are lovely, Sylvie,' Jean said sincerely, looking her up and down, dressed in a smart riding habit he had never seen before, consisting of a high-necked jacket and waistcoat in sky-blue, with a matching long skirt.

Her feathered hat sat high and firm on her auburn curls.

'Thank you, cousin,' she replied smiling, but there was a hint of tears in her eyes. 'I am sorry to be leaving you,' she said.

'Don't worry about me,' he replied. 'You'll have a marvellous time. And Elise will look after you, as will Yves.'

Sylvie could see he was becoming quite fond of his rival. She had to admit that she, too, was finding the marquis' company pleasant, although his arrogance was still a burden, an admission she would not have deigned to entertain two weeks ago. The thought of Yves waiting below for her made her heart race suddenly. But then she remembered his indelicacies regarding her mode of travel and her cheeks grew scarlet. The two-fold power Sainton had to attract, as well as to arouse the most indignant feelings in her, was extremely strange. She couldn't understand it, or herself.

'What's this?' Jean asked kindly, touching

her red cheeks. 'You're hot, Sylvie. You must not go if you have taken a fever. It would not be sensible to ride so far.'

'I am well. It must be excitement, or the fire,' Sylvie answered, putting her hand up to her forehead to cover her confusion.

'Quite so!' he said dryly. 'But are you really well?'

'I promise you I am, only extraordinarily apprehensive as to the expedition. And, of course, still worried about you.'

'I will come to no harm.' He smiled. 'I have good servants to guard me and you will not be gone long. Besides, I have learned my lesson and will not be careless in word or deed regarding my work in the future, also I have a great deal to do. Now that my private presentation has been well received by le Duc, I must get back to my drawing board. I have much time to catch up before the final.'

She could see he meant it. When there was work to be done, her cousin was single-minded.

'You will look after my horses?' Sylvie asked anxiously.

'Rest assured, my dear, they will not steal away on their own. Neither they, nor I, will be allowed to come to any harm. In any case, you have not that much intricate carving left to do, now you have finished the manes, and you need some little time for relaxation to renew your spirits. I'm sure a visit to Versailles will accomplish both.'

Jean hated Versailles with its miles of echoing corridors and its incessant intrigues, but he could see its excitement would appeal to any impressionable young woman.

'Now, are you sure you're ready?' he asked, as they reached the door. 'Elise and Yves will be waiting below.'

'All packed and ready to travel! I hope you have found me a suitable animal for such a long journey, Jean,' she said lightly.

His eyes twinkled at the tiny hint of anxiety which revealed itself in the question. He knew that Sylvie had no desire to appear a country cousin, but Elise had fixed it. And Jean, who was sad to lose Madame Baptiste as well as Sylvie, trusted his dear friend implicitly, knowing that, instinctively, she had come up with the right solution.

The noise in the courtyard was rising to almost unbearable levels as Sylvie and Jean descended the staircase. There was such a hustle and bustle of departure and arrival as carriages pulled in and out, bound for various parts. She found her whole body quivering with excitement as the carriage, evidently meant for their party, rolled into the cobbled space in front of them, its wheels clattering on the stones. Four chestnuts with plumes on their heads were pulling it and they appeared as excited as Sylvie felt. Yves came forward to greet her. He had been standing talking to

Elise, who was dressed in a purple cloak and a fur-trimmed tippet over a lavender travelling gown. Smiling, she took Jean's arm. Meanwhile, Yves' eyes wandered admiringly over Sylvie's person.

'You look enchanting,' he said.

'Thank you, my lord.'

He wore a dark brown greatcoat, which fell below knee level and was loose fitting with a vent at the back to facilitate riding. Underneath she glimpsed a sober brown cloth jacket, ending in half jackboots and spurs.

'You study me, Sylvie?'

'I beg your pardon,' she said. 'I was thinking about the journey'

She shook her head distractedly. Her fine apparel would be ill-suited to a mount of Pelotte's disposition! His dark eyes followed hers sympathetically. Then he gestured to a groom.

'Our mounts,' he ordered.

Elise, her arm linked in Jean's, walked over to them.

'So, the time is come,' she said.

Jean kissed her lightly on both cheeks, then turned to Sylvie to do the same.

'May God go with you, Sylvie, and you, madame,' he said.

She could see there were tears in his eyes.

'They'll be safe under my protection, Aubade,' Yves ventured.

A moment later, Elise and her maids were

settled in the carriage. Sylvie looked apprehensively across at the arch leading to the stables. Then she gasped. The most perfect horse she had ever seen was coming towards her.

'Oh, Jean,' she said, almost swooning with delight. 'Is he mine?'

To own an Arabian grey had been a dream of hers since childhood. It was so much like her marble animals. Yves' eyes twinkled with satisfied amusement as she rushed to meet the beautiful animal, patting its cheek excitedly, as the groom steadied its dainty head.

'Hello, my beauty,' she whispered. 'Thank you, thank you,' she called back. 'It's absolutely perfect. What is his name?' she asked the groom.

'Pegasus, mam'selle,' he replied.

'Pegasus,' she repeated, caressing his head even more to give him confidence and let him know she was his mistress. Then Yves came up.

'Although he has no wings, someone told me this one's gallop is as good as his breeding,' Yves said. 'I think he will give my Hesperus a run for his money.'

'I know he will,' Sylvie cried, her eyes gleaming.

Next moment, she was running over to Jean, kissing him. Moments later, she was mounted and looked down at Yves, who stood close to the toe of her riding boot. Now they were equal. He stared up into her face.

'I called you a goddess once. This morning you look like an angel.'

'Thank you, my Lord,' she said in a clear voice, settling the reins in her hand, 'but, remember, I ride like a devil.'

'So you mean to race me to Versailles?' he quipped, standing back.

Then, in a moment, he was springing into his saddle and bringing Hesperus' head round to join her mount's.

'You won't let her do anything too risky?' Jean called anxiously, as the two of them circled.

'Don't worry, Aubade. I will keep close to mam'selle.' Yves replied, leaning down. 'Hear that, Hesperus, we must keep up with Pegasus,' he whispered with a knowing smile.

Jean stood back, experiencing a mixture of feelings as he watched the two women dearest to him disappear from view.

'God speed,' he murmured as he turned away.

He would have been somewhat alarmed if he had seen a band of a dozen armed men ride out from behind the gates of the chateau to follow the little party as it made its way down the long drive in the direction of the forest and even more so, if he had noticed earlier on the darkly-sinister figure staring intently over the courtyard from an upstairs window marking the departure of the carriage as it lumbered slowly through the arch.

Guy de Barre rubbed his hands together and stared thoughtfully at them as he withdrew from the window of the upper chamber. No-one could accuse him of having their blood on his hands, but he had set the wheels in motion.

'This time, Sylvie, you will not elude me,' he hissed under his breath.

A moment later, he shouted for his servant and ordered him to alert Don Morales immediately to the fact that the Marquis of Sainton's party had just left the chateau.

Sylvie had a surprise in store, too. When they reached the crossroads near Chantilly, Yves called the little party to a halt.

'What are you doing?' she asked.

Yves was directing six of the armed men to take up their stations each side of Elise's carriage and beckoning the remaining to join them.

'Aren't we going all together?'

'I told your cousin I would take good care of you and Madame Elise,' he said, 'and it is better this way. Six of my men will accompany the carriage on one route, while you and I will take the rest another way. It is for safety's sake, and we will meet up on our first stop for the night.'

'I don't understand,' Sylvie cried, suddenly wary. 'Surely we would be better off staying close. Is there not safety in numbers?'

'Mam'selle,' Yves chided, his dark eyes

flashing, 'are you always so much trouble? A single carriage and six armed men is less obtrusive than a larger party of riders travelling together. It is my decision how I dispose of my soldiers. I begged you to ride with Madame Baptiste in the coach, but you refused. However, you can still change your mind if you wish.'

His eyes narrowed. Yves was taking no chances. Once they were in the forest's depths, it would be difficult for a large party to rally and escape, and he had no intention of leaving anyone behind. His armed guard was made up of twelve tough campaigners.

He was taking no chances with women in the party. His men had orders that should anything happen to him, they were to escort Mam'selle St Berthaud and Madame Baptiste singly to his home, west of Paris, where the ladies would be taken good care of. For this they would be handsomely recompensed with a sum, which no bribe could match.

In case they had any treacherous ideas, he had informed them they would be recompensed even further if he and the ladies reached their destination before nightfall. Yves had no illusions about men's greed and had made his plans extremely carefully. Soldiers fought better when they had something to fight for, and he intended to emerge from the forest alive!

But, at that moment, Yves did not want to

think of unpleasant matters. Today, he would have the freedom to talk to Sylvie as long as he wished. As the horses trotted off along the track, his last glance at Elise and her maids had revealed them lolling back against the cushions, enjoying the sun's warmth, ready to steal a few moments of slumber. Sylvie watched.

'Was madame happy with your decision to separate us?' she questioned.

'Yes, and in full agreement,' was the curt reply.

Sylvie bridled at his arrogance.

'But you did not consult me? Why?'

'Because, mam'selle, you would have questioned my judgement,' Yves returned directly, turning his horse's head in the direction of the sun. 'You have made your choice to stay with me, mam'selle. Come!'

Soon, Sylvie felt her temper abating and being replaced by excitement as they trotted along together amicably. As they talked, he found himself admiring everything about her, her lovely face and trim figure, the way she conversed and, in particular, the expert way she handled the frisky stallion on her first ride. But she must not know the true origin of the horse. Already he stood low in her estimation. She did not trust him, that was clear enough, but he was providing her with enough puzzles to take notice of him. And he would continue to do so, until his quest was complete.

They followed the leisurely route of the meandering River Oise in the direction of Royaumant Abbey.

'We shall not see the sanctuary,' Yves said, pointing out its direction with his whip, 'but it is a place dear to me.'

He spoke so fondly of the monks who had educated him that she was touched.

'Is Royaumont a very famous place then?' she asked.

'It is indeed. It is one of the greatest abbeys in France. The brothers were very good to me during my school days, but I missed home.'

This last speech was delivered with a regretful look, and Sylvie's heart warmed to the remark. She knew what it was like to be alone and friendless, and she desired to know much more about his parentage, and whether he was a true friend.

As the hours passed by, Yves could see his fair companion was tiring, but was too brave or stubborn to say so.

'We will pause very soon,' he said briefly.

It had been his intention not to stop until they had ridden a decent way enough from Chantilly to be less on their guard, and Yves was still being careful. But, in the forest, all was peaceful and still. Finally, they stopped to let their horses drink from the river, where the afternoon sun was making the water like a glittering rainbow.

With the horses tethered lightly and Sylvie

comfortably settled on a saddle cushion, Yves stretched out under a great lime, which threw its green canopy over their heads. The men-at-arms had been ordered to stand to at a distance and take only a morsel of food and wine, while they watered the horses.

'This is where we boys used to come and play on summer afternoons, when the monks released us from our studies. The river is shallow here and full of fish.'

Suddenly, she was imagining him as a handsome, dark-eyed child, playing in the water. It was a pleasant thought. He sat up and offered her a flagon of red wine, which she took gratefully, drinking a deep draught that revived her.

'You're pleased we have stopped? Are your bones aching? Mine are.'

'A little,' she said ruefully.

'Never mind,' he added. 'We will reach the chateau before nightfall, and then those pretty bones may rest,' he joked.

'It's very hot,' she said.

'Then you should undo that jacket. Don't worry, Sylvie,' he said. 'I won't tell Elise.'

'I do what I like, my lord,' she replied, rising to the challenge.

Next moment, she was unbuttoning the jacket, exposing her dainty waistcoat.

'Good,' he said, 'so do I!'

Seconds later, he had unbuckled his sword and laid it, glinting, on the grass. His brown riding coat was the next to be discarded to reveal his fine linen shirt was slashed at the neck. His eyes danced merrily as he caught her looking, then, next moment, he pitched himself forwards across the grass. He raised himself on his elbows to talk to her, looking for all the world like a peasant lad, instead of an aristocrat.

She took off her hat and leaned her back against the tree. The artist in her fancied that the two of them must look like some shepherd and his lass in a beautiful, painted landscape. Sylvie brushed back her hair from her forehead, which was wet with perspiration, glad he did not know what she was now thinking about his reputation. How many women had he loved? How many mistresses had he taken?

'I am so looking forward to some home comforts!' he exclaimed, turning on his back, a faraway look on his face.

'Is the chateau near home then?'

'It is my mother's house,' he replied in a dreamy voice. 'I have decided we will break our journey there. It will be far more pleasant than any inn.'

There was a smile on his lips as he closed his eyes against the sun and thought of taking Sylvie to meet his mother.

'Will she mind?'

'Maman is expecting us.'

Sylvie was surprised by the news. If Elise

had known they were going to stay for the night at his family home, why hadn't she told her? It was evident he stood high in Elise's and her cousin's estimation. But would he stand so high, if she had known he might betray them? She could not tell them! And what would his lady mother think of Sylvie? Was she used to her son bringing strange demoiselles to stay with her?

It was only after she asked herself that question she realised that, whatever his motives, she was eager to create the best impression possible on Madame Angèle, whom Elise had called a great lady, who doted so much on her son, she had removed to a house to be near him.

'You're very quiet, Sylvie,' Yves said, turning over again and touching the toe of her riding boot lightly.

Her strung-up nerves shivered at the contact. He got up and stretched his tall, lithe figure.

'I think you need your jacket on and, as you have no maid with you to help, I will.'

He picked it up, smiling and offered his limp arm to her. In reality, he had been desperate to touch her for the last hour, to pull her down beside him, feel her skin, to press his lips against hers and make those natural fears of hers dissolve for ever.

They took several seconds over putting on her jacket. His nearness as he kneeled beside her overwhelmed Sylvie. He exuded the scent of a gentleman, of leather and perfumed shaving soap, and he was so close, she could scarcely breathe.

'Sylvie,' he said.

His fingers reached out and touched a sky-blue button, brushing her thin waistcoat as he did so. She allowed him to start to fasten the troublesome buttons, but all her nature was straining for him, willing him not to close up her jacket, but to take her in his arms and press his chest against her. She had never felt quite like she did then, as if her senses had left her entirely.

'Yes, my lord?' she murmured in response, breathing quickly, looking up at him from under her lashes, laying him waste with her beauty.

'I think we must be gone if we are to reach the chateau before dark,' he said. 'Fasten your jacket yourself, I beg you. My hands are far too clumsy.'

Next moment, he was switching his eyes from hers, and rising to survey the landscape and cool his ardour. She faltered as she finished the task, her cheeks scarlet and her whole being suffused with angry disappointment at his brusque withdrawal and her own guilty imaginings.

A moment later, he was turning and offering his hand to help her rise, which she disdained. As she dusted grass and leaves off the skirt of her riding habit, he was watching her intently.

CHAPTER EIGHT

Madame Angèle's welcome and the gracious elegance of her house had been a wonderfully calming influence when, tired and nerve-racked, Sylvie had been helped down from Yves' horse later that evening. Although it was almost dark, her first impression of the place had been of a huge, creamy façade, lit by torches.

Madame Angèle was handsome, but not in a stiff, unapproachable way. Although her dress was elegantly trained, her headdress was not ridiculously large. Under it, her hair, streaked with grey, fell lightly over her rich, lace collar, and her dark eyes and curls were so much like her son's, that Sylvie had almost gasped. She remembered her words very clearly.

'Welcome to Maison Angelot, my dear.'

Then, Madame Angèle had extended her arms most graciously and, afterwards, Elise had hurried up to follow with her own greeting. Sylvie thought carefully over the happenings of the evening as a bell somewhere in the distance struck the eleventh hour. She sat quietly in her night attire, on the embroidered coverlet of the great four-poster.

She thought of how Yves and herself had been ushered into the grand salon and ordered to recount every tiny detail of their journey, which they did not! A wonderful dinner followed and elegant conversation, although Sylvie's head had been aching rather much to eat a good deal. But she had made a valiant effort to look as if she was intelligently alert. She did not want to appear flighty in front of Madame Angèle. It seemed to have worked because, after dessert, the lady's soft brown eyes had searched Sylvie's face tenderly.

'Sylvie, I had the very great pleasure of knowing your parents a little when they were at Versailles.'

'Thank you, madame,' Sylvie had curtsied.

Elise had been right. Yves' mother was indeed a great lady, but the epitome of serenity rather than worldliness. Sylvie would have liked to have carried on with the personal conversation. If Madame Angèle had known her mother she might add something to Sylvie's sketchy knowledge about everything, but at that moment Yves rose to embrace his mother fondly. Elise had embraced him warmly, too. In fact, she had continued to do so several times and most familiarly which, strangely, had unsettled Sylvie a great deal although she wasn't quite sure why.

Suddenly now, she recalled that night she had seen him in the garden of the chateau with a woman, probably his mistress. She felt the old anxieties rising. How was Jean managing without Sylvie to help him, and were her marble horses safe? Her mind jigged back and forth madly. Why had Elise not told her that they were to stay at Maison Angelot?

Suddenly, Guy de Barre's ugly face rose up in front of her. She was so distraught that she rose from the bed and wandered about the comfortable suite of rooms that had been placed at her disposal. Standing in the small dressing-room off her bedchamber, she realised suddenly she could hear the murmur of voices outside in the corridor. The man's tone was low, the woman was laughing lightly. What made Sylvie open the door warily was her recognition of both voices. She peeped through the crack and withdrew immediately.

Yves and Elise, who was wearing only a shawl over the lightest of negligees, were standing less than three yards from her. She was holding on to both his hands, chattering gaily and drawing him, smiling, into a neighbouring room. Sylvie stood motionless, a hot glow suffusing her face.

She rushed back into her bedroom and threw herself on the bed, feeling hot tears come into her eyes. So, the man had mistresses, but was Madame Elise one of those? Could it have been Elise with him that night at the chateau? If it was, then Sylvie could trust neither of them, as both were playing her false.

Suddenly, sense flew out of the window and she became so monstrously homesick for her chamber at Aubade that she pulled the pillow right over her head in disappointment and frustration. She felt she ought to return to Chantilly immediately, back home to Jean where she belonged and recount the sorry story that the two of them were being cheated.

Some moments later, she was aroused from her misery by a firm knocking. Who could be calling on her so late? She sniffed and wiped her eyes. Seconds later, she opened the door warily to reveal Yves!

'What are you doing here?' she exclaimed.

She knew she sounded peeved.

'I have your welfare at heart, remember. Madame Elise told me you were most preoccupied when she was with you earlier and I have called to see if you are still troubled.'

He looked so earnest she could have sworn he was sincere.

'I shall be no less troubled on account of your visit,' she replied haughtily.

'Do you intend to leave me standing here in the corridor?'

'Why should I not?' Sylvie snapped ungraciously. 'Doubtless there are many ladies who would be more than willing to let you into their chambers!'

'Fie, mam'selle,' he retorted. 'I assume by your temper you have just awakened, that you had already gone to your rest and I disturbed you!'

'It is not I who am ill-mannered. Do you always call on unchaperoned ladies at such late hours?'

'Only if they are very beautiful.'

Yves had recovered from her trouncing. Something was biting at her and he longed to know what it was. He had expected she would be asleep and not answer the door. Now he was extremely glad she had, having just emerged from another lady's chamber who, though privy to his secrets, caused his heart no turmoil.

He added mischievously, 'And, even more so, if her reputation is unimpaired, which it will not be, mam'selle,' he reminded, 'if I am seen standing at your chamber door. Let me in, please.'

Her tawny eyes flickered with alarm and Yves thought Sylvie looked even more like a goddess in her shift. He could not take his eyes off her.

'If you are so intent on compromising me and yourself, then come in,' she said.

Her cheeks were like poppies as he strode in. He stared over at the shallow shape her body had made on top of the coverlet of the four-poster.

'You were not asleep then. I take it that something has upset you?'

'How right you are, my lord,' she said,

turning her back on him.

'Turn to me, Sylvie, and tell me what is the matter.'

As she let him turn her lightly, his own senses reeled at her nearness. If ever a prize waited for some man, it would be this girl. Experience told him she felt like he was feeling. Yves ached as he looked into her eyes, longing to hold her body in his arms. But he had to be alert. Now she was shaking her head.

'You do not know?' she said.

She wanted to turn her back on him again but, now, he was holding on to her tightly. She struggled to free herself and he was forced to let her go.

'How dare you? I am not one of your women!' she pouted.

'One of my women? I don't know what you mean.'

'Don't sport with me, my lord. I know you have a mistress!'

'I have a mistress?' he repeated as tears were starting in her eyes. 'Many men have mistresses, Sylvie,' he chided, 'but, at present, I cannot say I am one of them.'

'At present!' she exploded, stamping her foot.

He frowned again then walked over to the fireplace, and, taking up the poker, thrust it into the dying embers, making them flare and spark. Then he swung round, tapping his forehead in sport.

'Ah, now I see! You are jealous, mam'selle?'

She gasped as he approached her like some prowling tiger.

'Indeed, I am not!'

She was breathing very hard.

'And my arrogance offends you?'

He stopped, telling himself he should not tease her.

'Keep away, sir.'

'Are you accusing me of having a mistress or wanting one?'

'Don't come any nearer, sir,' she gasped, 'or I'll . . .'

Her eyes were searching for something with which to defend herself. She could feel his warm breath as he whispered his reply.

'Will what? Hit me with the candlestick?'

A second later, he was taking her in his arms. Sylvie's head was dizzy with shame as she felt her eager body respond to Yves' embrace in a fashion she had only imagined in her dreams. Then she found herself struggling against a passion welling up inside her, which she had never experienced before.

'No, no, Yves,' Sylvie moaned. 'Please, Yves, please let me go!'

She was too afraid of her feelings. Yves' brain fought with emotions. Finally, his conscience suddenly struggled free.

'Forgive me, mam'sellle, I beg your pardon with all my heart.'

She didn't answer, only clung to him.

'I'm sorry,' he added.

'So am I,' she said, wresting herself out of his arms, trembling all over.

'I did not come here to . . .' he began.

'Don't! Don't speak,' she stammered.

She felt hopeless about it all. Did he think so little of her that he had defied convention and come to her chamber in his mother's house?

'I think you should go now,' she said, but her voice had not the imperious tone she wished, but came out hurt and broken.

Emptiness and a horrid cold suffused her body, too! She had let him be her champion, her accuser and, just now, her suitor—and he was a fraud! He must be. He had just emerged from another woman's room. Elise was cheating on her cousin, and also, Yves was allied with Guy de Barre, her tormentor, who had sworn to ruin them both unless she succumbed to him.

'I want you to go. Now,' she said in hushed tones.

Had Sylvie been more experienced she would have realised that cruelly cheating one's heightened senses always brought about a callous response.

'Very well, mam'selle, but I do not want you to think less of me for this.'

'I could not think less of you,' she replied quietly.

'Then we are friends still?'

Her heart lurched. She was searching for the right words. No, she couldn't hate him. She knew that, whatever he had done.

'It serves no purpose to examine our acquaintance, sir,' she said. 'Let us remain as we were before.'

'Very well, and, good-night, Sylvie. Sleep well.'

Suddenly, Yves needed to be away. Next moment, he was padding to the door, relieved he had been able to control himself. To take her would have been unforgivable.

When he had gone, Sylvie lay on the bed and buried her face in the pillow. What was a man? Was this one so insensitive that he didn't know how much damage he had done? How could she sleep well? Her heated senses had been fuelled by the magnificence of his body, by the way his hungry mouth searched hers. Sleep well? Sylvie felt she would never sleep again without remembering!

They left his mother's house at seven in the morning. It had been an uncomfortable night for Sylvie, given what had happened in her bedchamber. She was downcast and both Elise and Angèle had remarked on the fact when she left.

'I am very tired,' she had excused herself.

She was surprised to learn that Elise was not to accompany them farther, having said she would follow later. Suddenly, Sylvie was wary. Yves had little to say that morning. There were unnatural dark shadows below his eyes and his lips were set in a hard line. Sylvie knew he was offended, but his behaviour the night before had been quite unforgivable.

They trotted along disconsolately, both lost in a world of their own, but a detached observer would have seen that Yves' dark eyes were supremely watchful. Not far from Versailles, what Yves had feared began to happen. A party of riders was following them. The horsemen were riding hard, their beasts' hooves drumming the earth. They were too far away to be recognisable, but too near for safety's sake. Hercule and Pegasus caught their unfamiliar scent and began neighing excitedly.

'Who are they?' Sylvie asked, realising from the look on Yves' face that they faced danger.

'I'm not sure,' Yves said, 'but they're coming too fast at us to be up to any good.'

He barked curt orders to the men-at-arms.

'But what can I do?' Sylvie began.

'Just do as you're told,' he replied imperiously.

Gone were the courtesies, the soft words of last night. Sylvie bridled at such added high-handedness, but her common sense took over. She obeyed swiftly and dug her heels into Pegasus' side. The horse responded. As she gave him his head, she could see their men-at-arms already turning to face the strangers. A moment later, they were engaged in a fierce battle, filling the spaces between the trees with the horrid sound of the clash of blades.

'Go!' Yves commanded, turning to help. 'Go, Sylvie! Ride!'

Sylvie went cold all over. The sound of screams curdled her blood. She kicked the horse's sides mercilessly, thanking God she was not riding old Pelotte. Next moment, she could hear the heavy drum of hoof beats gaining on her. Was it Yves or them? She didn't turn her head, but rode on frantically. Next moment, a rider, eyes burning madly above the red-fringed scarf, which doubled as a mask, drew level.

'Keep your hands off me, villain!' Sylvie screamed, plucking out her whip.

She rained down blows on his face and shoulders.

'Vixen!' her assailant snarled.

A moment later, his gloved hand had the whip tight and was wresting it from her. Pegasus was forced to slow down as the two galloping mounts were brought dangerously close. Sylvie still hung on to her whip gamely, praying inwardly. Then he prised it from her and threw it away. Suddenly, he was clawing and ripping at the skirt of her riding habit, trying to slow her down, to unseat her.

She could hear the stout fabric tearing as she continued to resist valiantly, the back of her knee clamped so tightly around the saddle horn that it pained her dreadfully. But neither rider had noticed the heavy tree branch strung right across their path. A second later, both hit it and were thrown from their saddles. They each struck the forest floor hard and lay apart, winded by their fall. Then, as a dazed and gasping Sylvie came to, she felt the man launch himself on top of her again, trying to pinion her arms!

She fought like a wild animal savagely fights for survival against the hunter. But his strength was much greater and the reserves she had drawn from deep within her were ebbing. Finally, he had her on her back and was mercilessly dragging her arms to her sides to pinion her.

'Get off, you brute,' she screamed, spitting in his face.

He responded by letting go her arms. She grabbed at a piece of wood, which had broken off the heavy branch and, miraculously, lay near her hand. Sylvie struck upwards with the force of a lioness and smashed the stick hard against his forehead. The man shouted out in agony. She fell back exhausted. Then, she blacked out . . .

She came to in a cold sweat and found herself blinking dizzily into a man's face.

'No!' she screamed, flailing desperately with her arms.

'It's all right. You're safe!'

'Yves!'

She sobbed with relief, staring up into his dark eyes.

'Did I kill him?' she whispered in a small, cracked voice.

'No.'

She tried to rise.

'Not yet,' he repeated and she felt his hands moving swiftly over her.

'Don't, please,' she remonstrated weakly, putting two trembling hands up to still his.

'I told you not to move!' he ordered.

She felt him gently pulling across the fabric of her torn habit.

'No broken bones,' he added.

'Who were they?'

'Sh, chèrie!' he advised anxiously. 'Lie still, save your breath.'

As he bent close over her, Sylvie's horrified eyes realised that Yves' linen shirt was no longer white. Dark red blood was oozing from an open gash in his chest. She fainted again. Yves cradled Sylvie in his arms. His anger was waning, leaving behind a stiff coldness in the place where the sword point had torn into his flesh. The only emotion left in him now was grateful relief she was still alive. Her attacker would pay in more ways than one.

'Mam'selle, you have some courage,' he murmured, looking down at her milk-white face.

He turned to see his victorious men-at-arms come riding up.

'Over here,' he shouted.

He had no compassion for any of the others

who, in threatening his life, had lost theirs or lay wounded. Sylvie's attacker had been a Spaniard. The brute was trussed as tightly as a capon for the oven, blubbering he was ready to talk, to give evidence. What fate would have been Sylvie's at the hands of such assassins?

Yves shivered. He was glad it was over. He had been made to pose as the friend of the most vile and loathsome man in the whole of France. That man had gambled and lost. Now he would pay for his sins at last.

Next moment, protected by a circle of his soldiers, Yves held a small vial of smelling salts under Sylvie's nose, attempting to revive her. She spluttered violently as the smell claimed her senses.

'My head,' she moaned, staring blankly around her.

'Come,' Yves said, lifting her to her feet. 'How are you feeling? Are you fit enough to ride behind me?'

Sylvie tottered as he put her down, bones aching.

'The quicker we put this forest and its dangers behind us, the better.'

Next moment, Yves was up in his saddle and she felt herself being heaved into the air by two men-at-arms. It was no time to worry about her dignity. Once seated astride behind him, she could do nothing but cling to his back. He looked over his shoulder, his own face pale from loss of blood. He had no time to wait. His wound was deeper than he had first thought.

'Hang on tight, and try not to worry!'

She obeyed without a word, although her head was full of questions, shouting for answers. But it was not the time to ask, only to listen, obey and pray they reach some safe harbour before nightfall.

CHAPTER NINE

They did find safety and now one whole month had passed at Versailles. Also, thanks to Yves, the day Sylvie had waited for the whole of her life had come at last. The gratitude she felt towards the marquis she had so stoutly mistrusted swelled within her fit to burst.

Since that night in her bedchamber at his mother's house, Yves had spoken no words of passionate love to her, only treated her like a tender flower. Now, she looked across the great, glittering room, full of the noblemen and women of France. Their heads nodded at her. She had been whispered about throughout the Court as her sad story unfolded.

She felt breathless as she stared at the splendid velvet dais, the gilded chairs, the empty throne. They were waiting for Louis XV and Yves, his beloved companion, and Sylvie was to be presented to the boy King. Her superb white gown encrusted with jewels almost dragged her down, but her heart was light. Her ridiculously-large head dress wobbled when she walked but she had practised enough in it to still be graceful.

It was all like a dream, and yet, dear Elise, about whom her suspicions had been unfounded, and Yves' dear mother, Angèle, were at her side. There, also, was her cousin, Jean, summoned to attend. He had been persuaded by Elise to discard his simple clothes and don the grandest velvet and ruffles he had ever seen. Monsieur le Duc had accompanied him on the journey from Chantilly, but, of course, le Duc was with the King at that moment, accorded his rightful place. They were all here for her!

But what mattered most was that Sylvie was now safe, in the great palace from which her father, Leon, had fled, disgraced. She was here to take her rightful place, not as a poverty-stricken noblewoman, but as a sorely-injured lady, who could proudly acknowledge her parents' real worth.

She could hardly believe still that it had been the young monarch himself who had instigated the whole inquiry into the matter of her lost estates, her oppression by de Barre and attempted abduction. Yves had actually been sent by him to spy on de Barre and, what was even more amazing, Elise was a spy, too! Now, the day of the monster's judgment had come.

How Elise had laughed when she had found out Sylvie thought she was Yves' mistress.

'My dear, he would never look at me,' she said. 'He has eyes for one woman only.'

Sylvie had desperately wanted to ask if she meant her, but she could not. It would not have been decent.

Then the trumpets sounded and all around her courtiers were bowing stiffly. Sylvie's bedazzled eyes were fixed upon the small procession led by a handsome young boy in a luxurious, curly wig, dressed in white silk and bedecked with jewels. A heavy, purple velvet cloak trimmed with the finest ermine trailed behind him. He seated himself on the gilded throne.

'Your Majesty,' she murmured, recovering from her curtsey.

As she lifted her eyes, they were met with a glance from wise, dark ones. And Yves was beside the boy, whispering and smiling.

'Come forward, Mademoiselle St Berthaud,' the King ordered in a clear, high voice.

The company gasped as she moved.

'Yes, up, up the steps. Here.'

A footman escorted her to a chair two steps lower than the canopied throne. Then Yves was beside her, his body exuding strength and warmth, giving her courage. She listened in a daze as His Majesty spoke of the wrongs which had been done to her. The charges were read out by a stem gentleman in black. She could not have borne it all if Yves' strong fingers had not been pressing her shoulder.

Then the man she hated above all men entered. She didn't want to look at him, but when she forced herself, he was not the same de Barre who had threatened her all her life. He now wore the look of a whipped dog. The jewels had gone and the strutting manners. Now he shuffled like an old man, but she could not be sorry for him.

Her heart only lifted when sentence was passed. The King had been merciful, banishing him for life. When he was led away she was near to fainting. But there was greater happiness to come.

At the reception in her honour, the King announced news that made her tremble with joy. She looked up at Monsieur le Duc, who was standing with her proud cousin, Jean, whose tribulations were also over.

'Your cousin has the commission for the stables, mam'selle. There was no-one in France, nay in Europe, who could surpass his skills, and, to crown this day, I have chosen your fine horses to adorn my gates.'

When the King joined them, Sylvie felt too overwhelmed to speak.

'Great Condé tells me your marble beasts are the talk of France. I am jealous,' he said. 'I think I will keep you here in Versailles to design a fountain for me.'

His eyes were full of fun.

'And Yves, too. You both must stay and keep me company.'

They bowed. But Jean's eyes were sorrowful.

King Louis was wise for his tender years, adding, 'But only for a time. Then you may return to your cousin in Chantilly. He has great need of you.'

'Thank you, sire,' Jean replied. 'Sylvie is everything to me.'

'I'm sure she is,' the King added. 'But you have Madame Elise to comfort you. When she has finished my portrait, I will release her, too.'

Elise's eyes were sparkling. Sylvie knew it was Elise's greatest desire to paint the King. He had been so good to all of them. How had she ever thought she was an unfortunate girl? Now there was only one thing she desired—to make amends to Yves. She had not trusted him and she was sorry. She had been so silly, and he had been unnaturally silent of late. Maybe he was angry with her. But they were to stay at Versailles together. Would he forgive her? If he did not, it would break her heart.

Sylvie had realised some time ago she had fallen in love with Yves, but her pain stemmed from the fact she did not know if he loved her. But she remembered his ardour in the bedchamber at his mother's house. Would he ever talk so again? She found that she did not blush at the thought any more. All the traumas of the past months had made her grow up.

The wonderful day flitted by like a dream. Sylvie couldn't sleep properly after all the excitement. She turned over and over on her pillow, tormented by the strangest dreams. She came to fully in the early hours. She realised she had left the bed drapes only half pulled. Outside, the moonlight shone up the grey, stone walls, silvering them and her windowsill. She rose and walked, shivering, over to the window.

She had an urgent instinct to dash out there into the silence, and drink in nature's beauty. How she longed for Chateau Aubade and home, for the song of the nightingales and the soft breezes blowing about her room in the tower. She did not want to be alone.

Pulling on a warm cloak over her negligee, she hurried down the stairs and out into the garden. In the distance, she could see torches flickering. There must be others out in the palace gardens, too, probably lovers meeting, poets composing verses, but she was all alone. Then she heard footsteps close behind. She was still nervous although there was nothing to fear any more.

'Mam'selle?'

The tones were rich and soft. She knew that voice.

'My lord,' she said, lifting her face towards Yves. 'How did you know I was here?'

'I could not sleep either, Sylvie. I was pacing in my bedroom, when the moonlight reminded me that there is beauty outside, too.'

'Were you anxious, sir?'

She half-hoped it could have been thoughts of her that kept him awake, but she dismissed them as vanity. Yves felt himself stir when he looked in her eyes. They were innocent, but he remembered the burning looks she had given him when they had danced at the chateau. He had held that picture of her deep in his heart.

He added mischievously, 'I have something on my mind, which I can confide to no-one.'

Her tawny eyes flickered with much alarm. Yves thought Sylvie looked like a startled fawn or a gorgeous spirit of the night. How he yearned to touch and caress the shyness out of her.

'You can trust me,' she answered.

Her cheeks burned at her daring, but she knew the moonlight would hide her flush.

'Can I? It's the greatest secret any man can bear.'

His senses reeled at her nearness. His experience told him she was testing the waters, trying him out, daring him to declare himself. Once again, he thought if ever a prize waited for some man, it would be this girl. Yves longed to take her in his arms. She was nodding.

'Please tell me,' she said. 'Maybe I can help.'

'Perhaps you can, but my arrogance might

offend you. It has before.'

He stopped, chiding himself for teasing her.

'That was before I knew you properly, sir.'

'And you know me now? Once you accused me of having a mistress. You pressed me hard, Sylvie, and I lied when I said I didn't have one.'

'I see.'

Her heart lurched and a great disappointment filled her. Yves had someone after all, and now he was going to tell her about it.

'Do you still want to know?' he asked.

'I think so,' she said uncertainly, feeling his warm breath.

'Then I will tell you, Sylvie. You shall be the first to know my secret.'

The air around her was thick with anticipation as she waited.

'I am in love.'

'In love?'

She could feel herself trembling. If only it was with her! A second later, he took her in his arms and she crumpled against his chest with relief.

'With you, Sylvie. It was always you.'

'Was it? I thought . . . thought . . . you despised me!'

'You little goose,' he said. 'I have cared for you since the very first time we met and you gave me short shrift in the forest. You were magnificent, Sylvie, and I confess, I teased you shamefully. And when I found out that Guy de Barre . . .'

'Don't speak of him,' she almost whispered.

'All right, I won't. Just kiss me, Sylvie, and be mine!'

Now she knew he was sincere and she surrendered totally to his kisses.

'Hold me, Yves, hold me close!' she murmured, almost afraid of her feelings as she clung to him.

A woman could deny him nothing. Then he let her go. Taking her hand, he lifted it to his lips.

'I have something to ask you,' he said. 'Would you do me the honour of becoming my wife?'

The words rang in her ears triumphantly. He wanted to marry her, not make her his mistress! She sighed with relief.

'You know I will,' she answered, without hesitation, 'if you are sure.'

'I am quite, quite sure,' he said. 'I was afraid you would say no!'

The wind carried their laughter across the gardens.

'Now let us go in,' Yves said, cradling her to him, 'and in the morning, I can divulge my secret to the world. It has made me ache so long.'

'Please, Yves, don't let's go in yet,' Sylvie cried, 'but rather take a turn in the garden before the moon disappears behind those clouds.'

They strolled on hand in hand through the maze of box hedges until they paused by a fountain.

'What are you thinking, Sylvie?' Yves asked softly, as she stood quietly with her head against his shoulder.

'I was thinking that three more marble horses would look wonderful right there,' she answered quaintly.

He let out a peal of laughter.

'I am marrying a sculptress indeed. And I'm glad.'

He kissed her lips again.

'Now, no more talk of horses, mam'selle. It is the early hours. I will see you to your chamber and perhaps this night you will not leave me quite as cruelly as before.'

'I think I will not,' she said playfully as they turned, hand in hand, towards the doorway to the palace—and happiness together.